The Graphic Novel Adventures of Sherlock Holmes

Sir Arthur Conan Doyle's

The Adventure of the Six Napoleons

Adapted by: Vincent Goodwin

Illustrated by: Ben Dunn

magic wagon

visit us at
www.abdopublishing.com

Published by Magic Wagon, a division of the ABDO Group, PO Box 398166, Minneapolis, Minnesota, 55439. Copyright © 2014 by Abdo Consulting Group, Inc. International copyrights reserved in all countries. All rights reserved. No part of this book may be reproduced in any form without written permission from the publisher.

Graphic Planet™ is a trademark and logo of Magic Wagon.

Printed in the United States of America, North Mankato, Minnesota.
042013
092013

 This book contains at least 10% recycled materials.

Written by Sir Arthur Conan Doyle
Adapted by Vincent Goodwin
Illustrated by Ben Dunn
Colored by Robby Bevard
Lettered by Doug Dlin & Robby Bevard
Edited by Stephanie Hedlund and Rochelle Baltzer
Interior layout by Antarctic Press
Cover art by Ben Dunn
Cover design by Abbey Fitzgerald

Library of Congress Cataloging-in-Publication Data

Goodwin, Vincent.
  Sir Arthur Conan Doyle's The adventure of the six Napoleons / adapted by Vincent Goodwin ; illustrated by Ben Dunn.
     p. cm. -- (The graphic novel adventures of Sherlock Holmes)
  Summary: Retold in graphic novel form, Sherlock Holmes is called in to solve the mystery of the Napoleon busts, which are being stolen only to be immediately smashed to pieces.
  ISBN 978-1-61641-976-9 | ISBN 978-1-62402-999-8 (pbk)
1. Doyle, Arthur Conan, Sir, 1859-1930. Adventure of the six Napoleons--Adaptations. 2. Holmes, Sherlock (Fictitious character)--Comic books, strips, etc. 3. Holmes, Sherlock (Fictitious character)--Juvenile fiction. 4. Graphic novels. [1. Graphic novels. 2. Doyle, Arthur Conan, Sir, 1859-1930. Adventure of the six Napoleons--Adaptations. 3. Mystery and detective stories.] I. Dunn, Ben, ill. II. Doyle, Arthur Conan, Sir, 1859-1930. Adventure of the six Napoleons. III. Title. IV. Title: Adventure of the six Napoleons.
  PZ7.7.G66Siri 2013
  741.5'973--dc23
                                                          2013004377

Table of Contents

Cast

Sherlock Holmes

Dr. John Watson

Beppo

Dr. Barnicot

Mr. Josiah Brown

Mr. Gelder

Mr. Harding

Morse Hudson

Inspector Lestrade

Mr. Sandeford

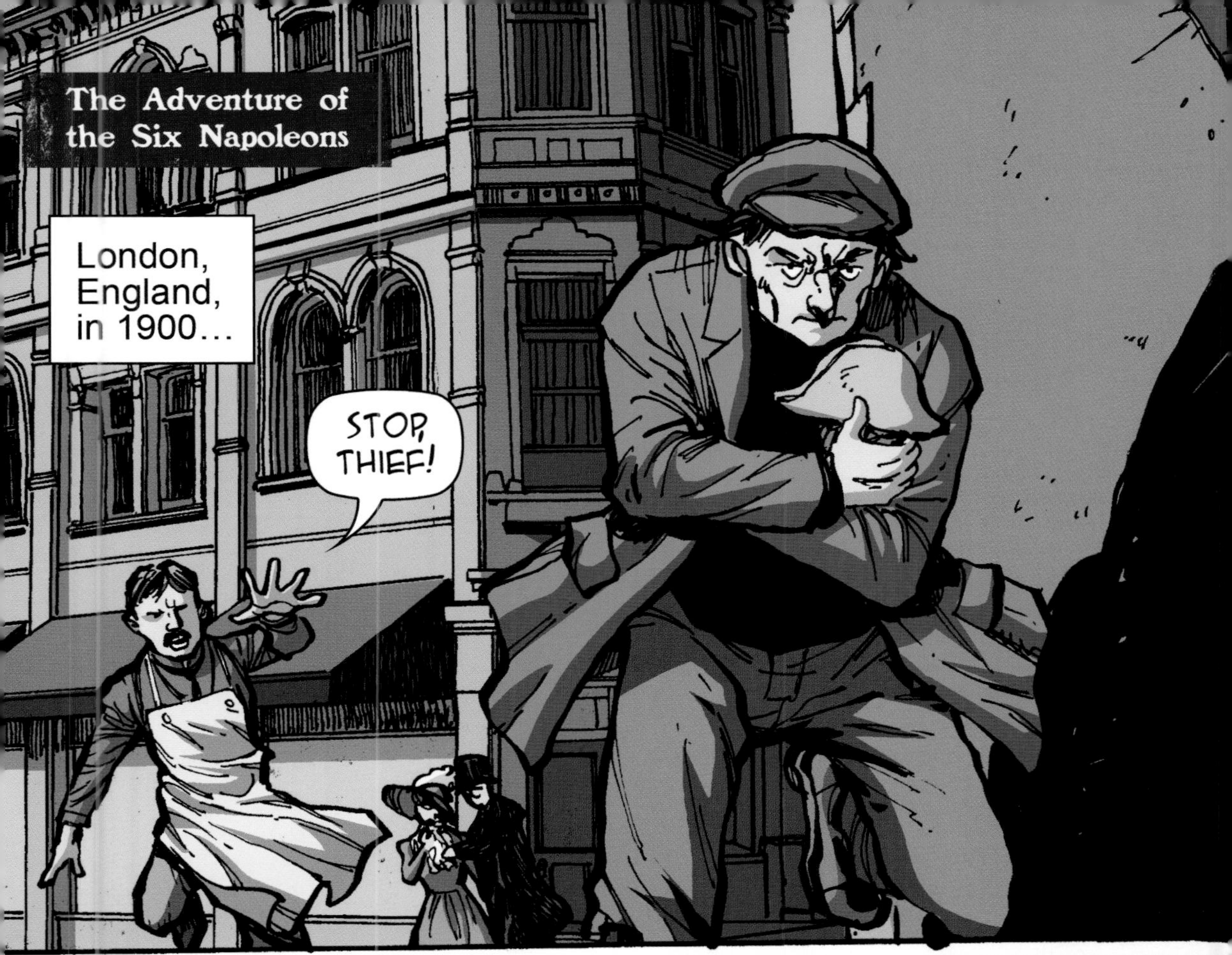
The Adventure of the Six Napoleons
London, England, in 1900…
STOP, THIEF!

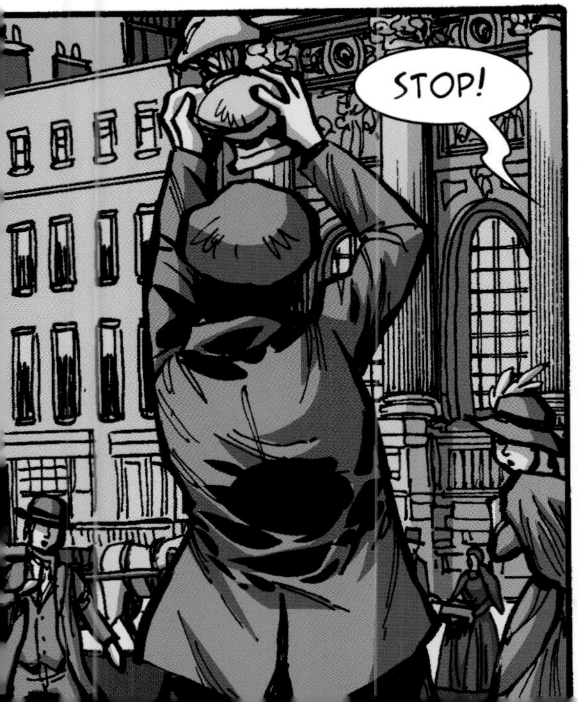
STOP!

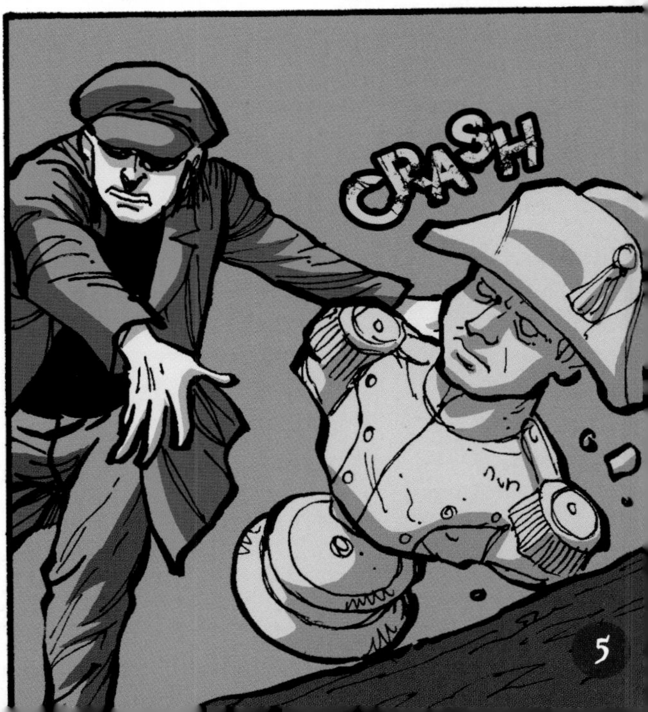
CRASH

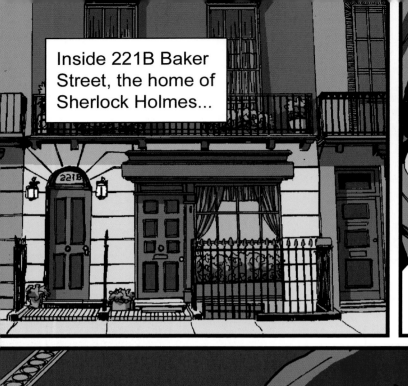

Inside 221B Baker Street, the home of Sherlock Holmes...

FOUR DAYS AGO, MORSE HUDSON REPORTED A ROBBERY FROM HIS ART SHOP.

WAS THE ITEM VALUABLE?

NO, THAT'S THE THING.

THE STORE WAS FULL OF EXPENSIVE ITEMS, BUT THE THIEF ONLY TOOK THE NAPOLEON BUST. IT WAS NOT WORTH MORE THAN A FEW SHILLINGS.

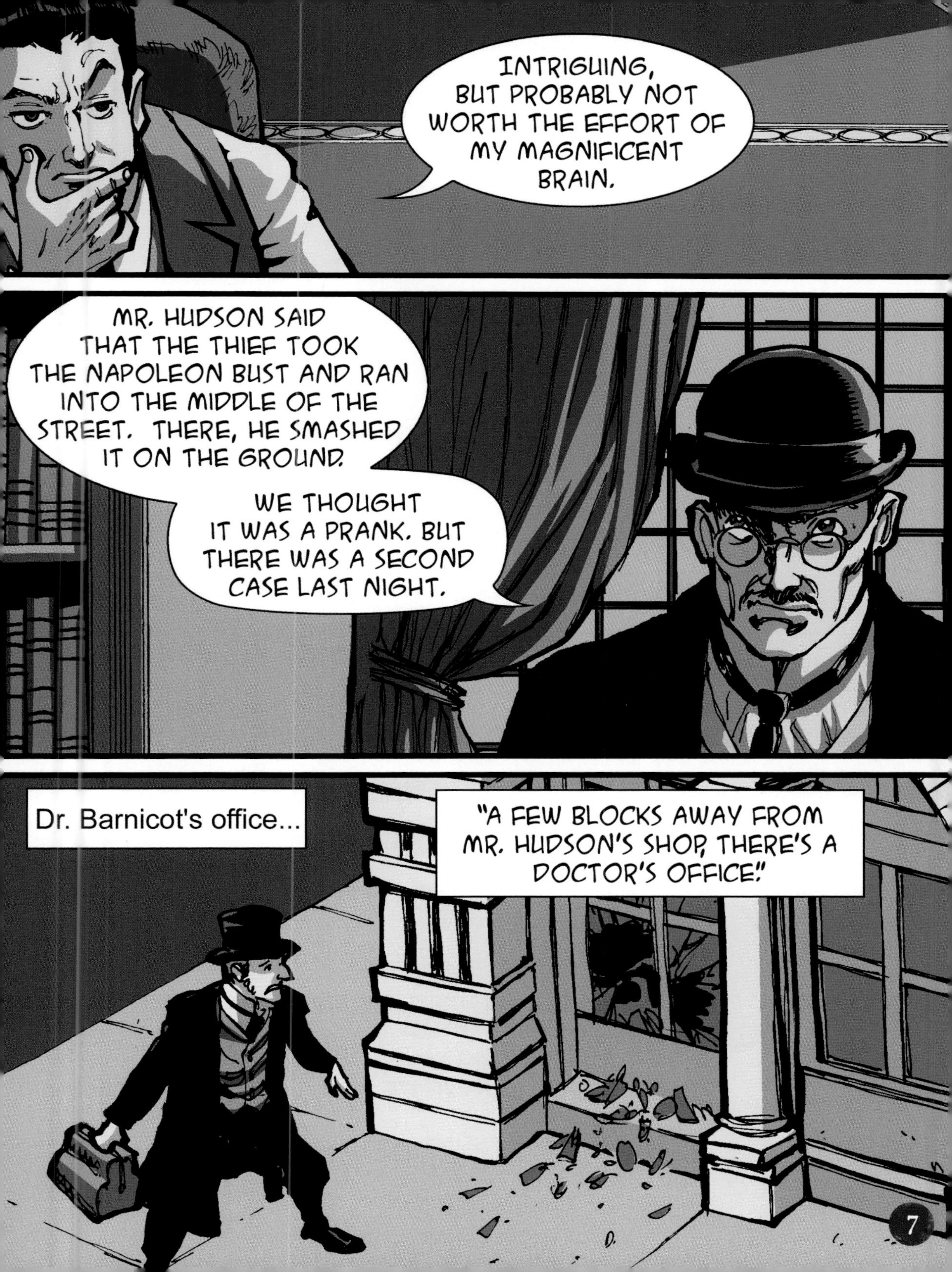
INTRIGUING, BUT PROBABLY NOT WORTH THE EFFORT OF MY MAGNIFICENT BRAIN.
MR. HUDSON SAID THAT THE THIEF TOOK THE NAPOLEON BUST AND RAN INTO THE MIDDLE OF THE STREET. THERE, HE SMASHED IT ON THE GROUND.
WE THOUGHT IT WAS A PRANK. BUT THERE WAS A SECOND CASE LAST NIGHT.
Dr. Barnicot's office...
"A FEW BLOCKS AWAY FROM MR. HUDSON'S SHOP, THERE'S A DOCTOR'S OFFICE."

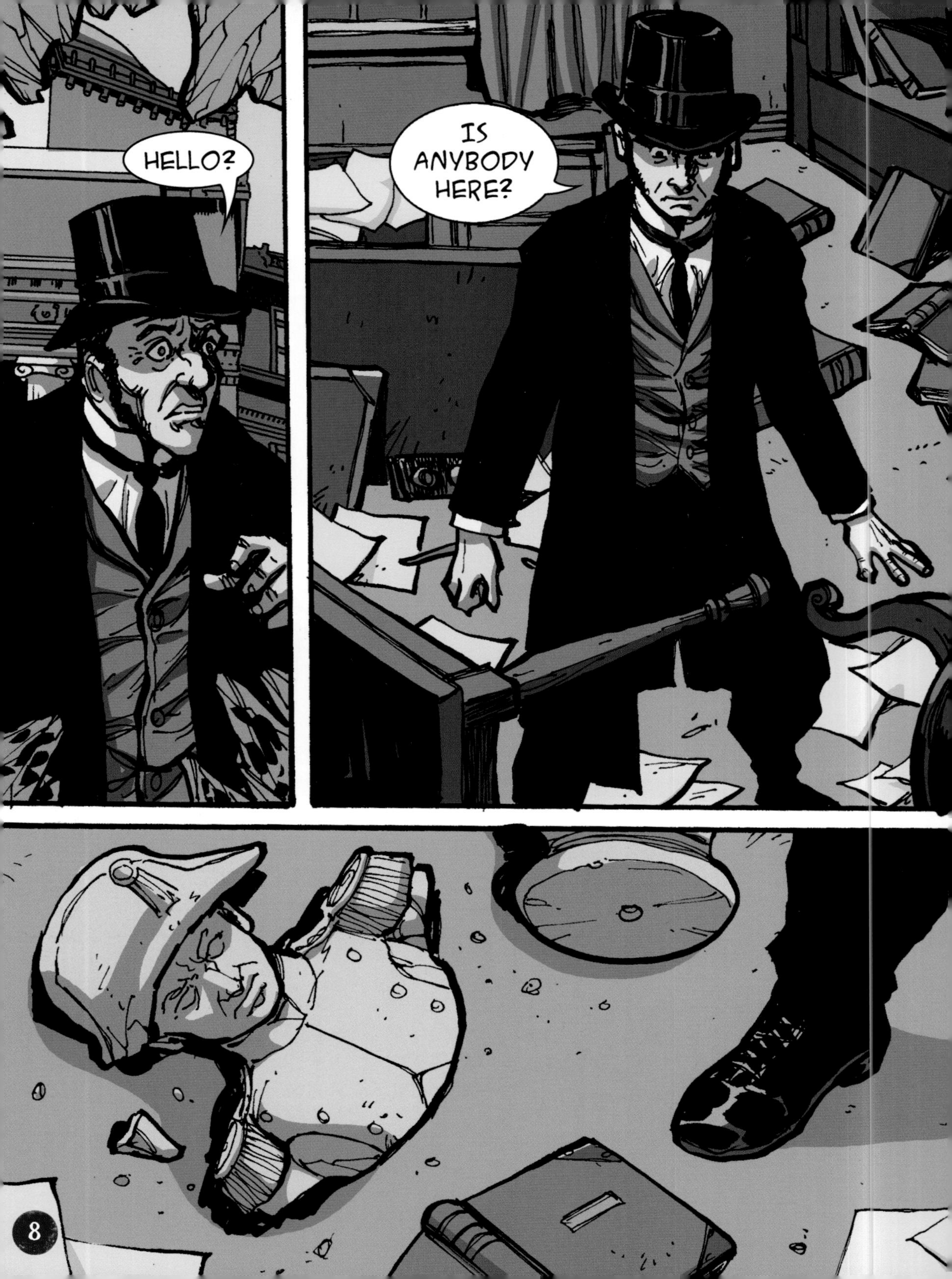
HELLO?
IS ANYBODY HERE?

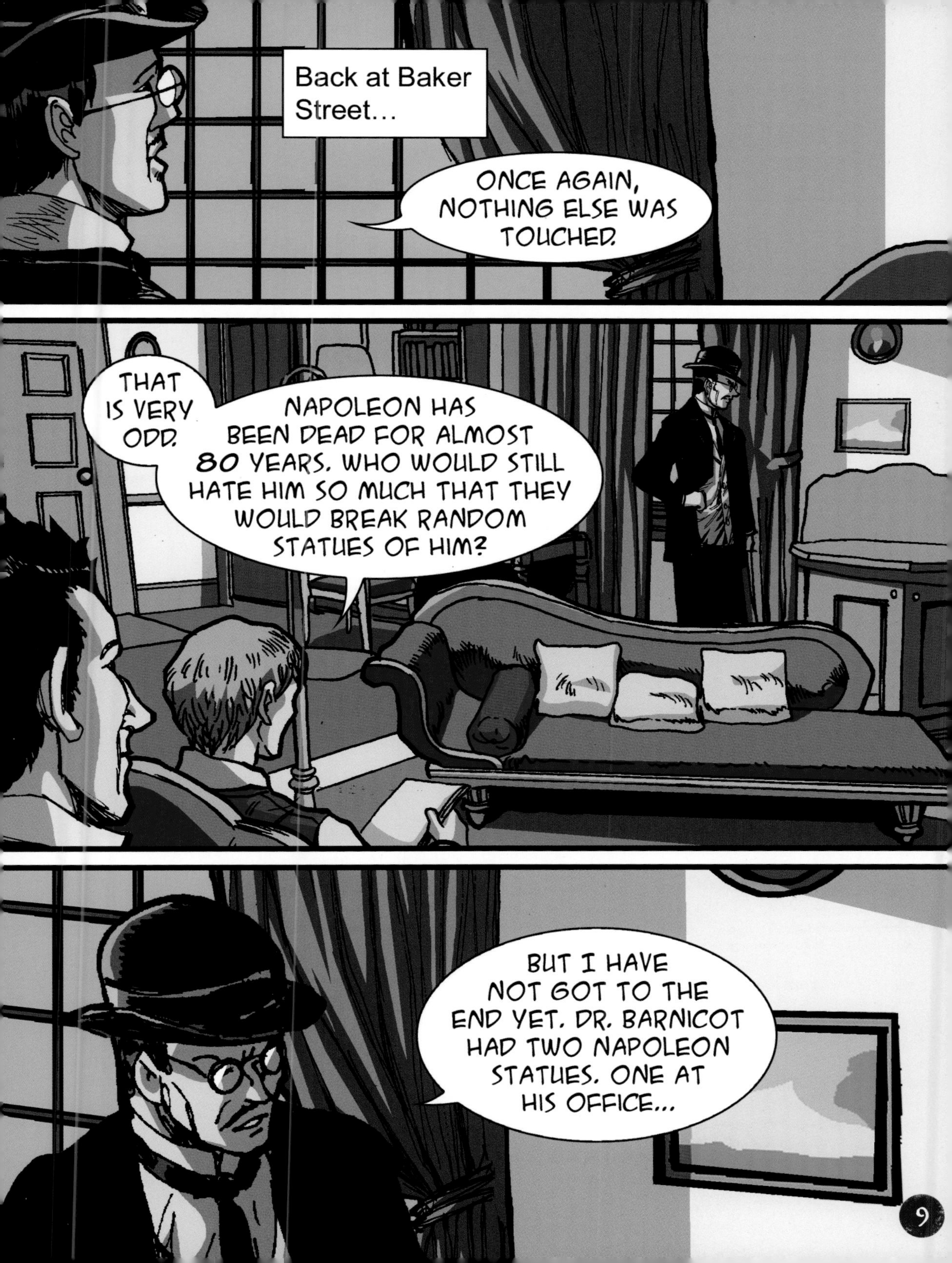
Back at Baker Street...
ONCE AGAIN, NOTHING ELSE WAS TOUCHED.
THAT IS VERY ODD.
NAPOLEON HAS BEEN DEAD FOR ALMOST 80 YEARS. WHO WOULD STILL HATE HIM SO MUCH THAT THEY WOULD BREAK RANDOM STATUES OF HIM?
BUT I HAVE NOT GOT TO THE END YET. DR. BARNICOT HAD TWO NAPOLEON STATUES. ONE AT HIS OFFICE...

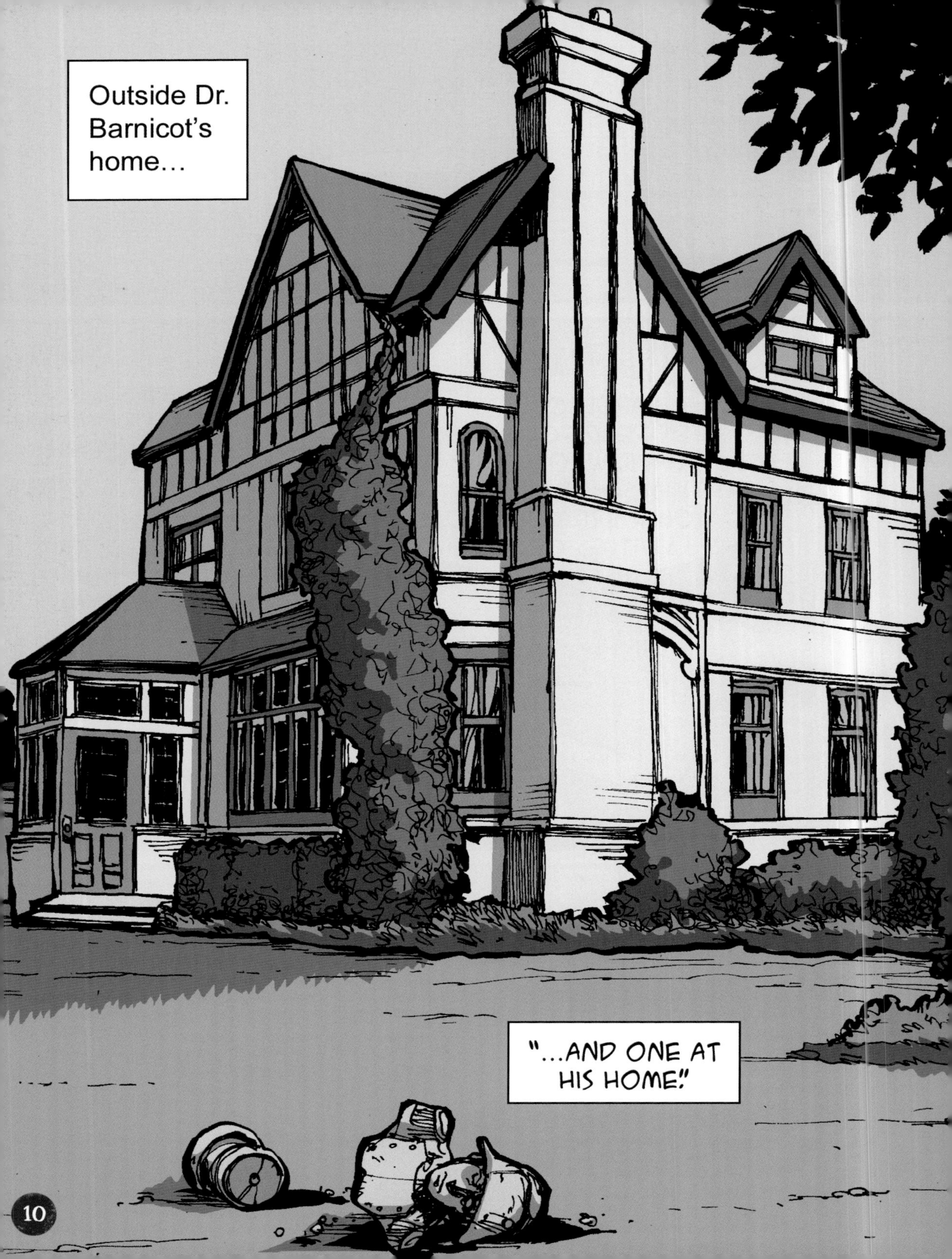
Outside Dr. Barnicot's home…
"…AND ONE AT HIS HOME!"

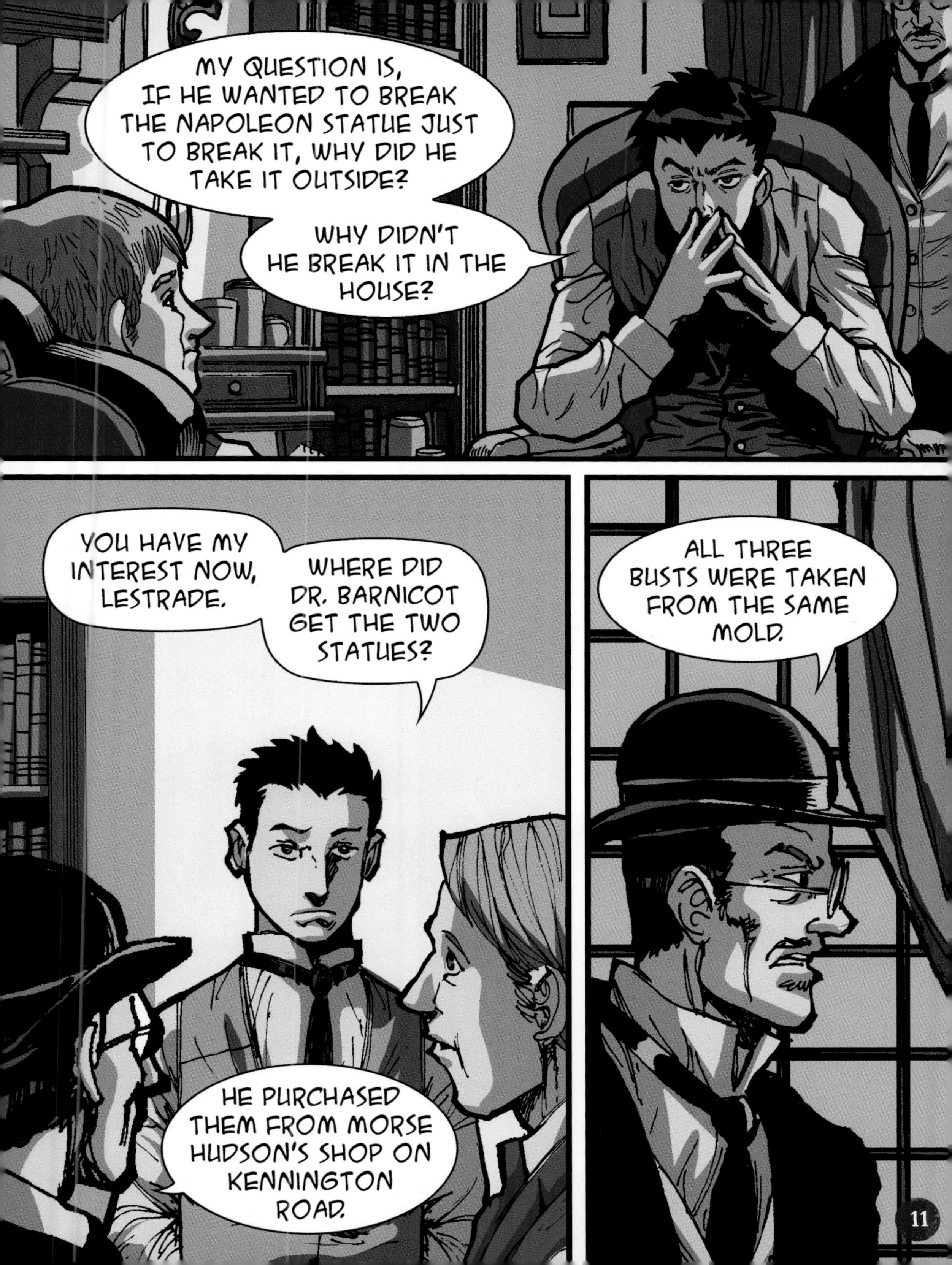
MY QUESTION IS, IF HE WANTED TO BREAK THE NAPOLEON STATUE JUST TO BREAK IT, WHY DID HE TAKE IT OUTSIDE?
WHY DIDN'T HE BREAK IT IN THE HOUSE?
YOU HAVE MY INTEREST NOW, LESTRADE.
WHERE DID DR. BARNICOT GET THE TWO STATUES?
HE PURCHASED THEM FROM MORSE HUDSON'S SHOP ON KENNINGTON ROAD.
ALL THREE BUSTS WERE TAKEN FROM THE SAME MOLD.

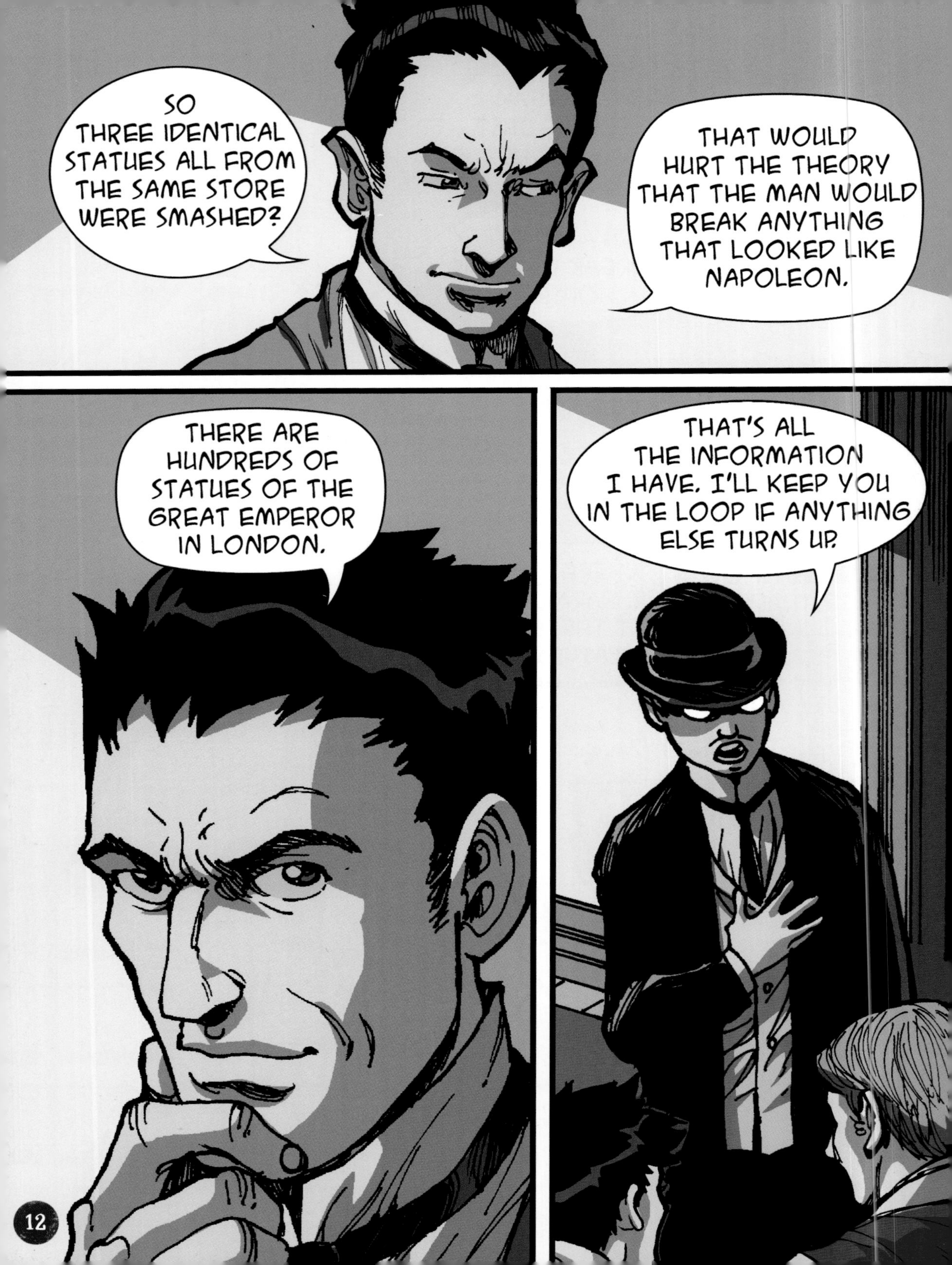
SO THREE IDENTICAL STATUES ALL FROM THE SAME STORE WERE SMASHED?
THAT WOULD HURT THE THEORY THAT THE MAN WOULD BREAK ANYTHING THAT LOOKED LIKE NAPOLEON.
THERE ARE HUNDREDS OF STATUES OF THE GREAT EMPEROR IN LONDON.
THAT'S ALL THE INFORMATION I HAVE. I'LL KEEP YOU IN THE LOOP IF ANYTHING ELSE TURNS UP.

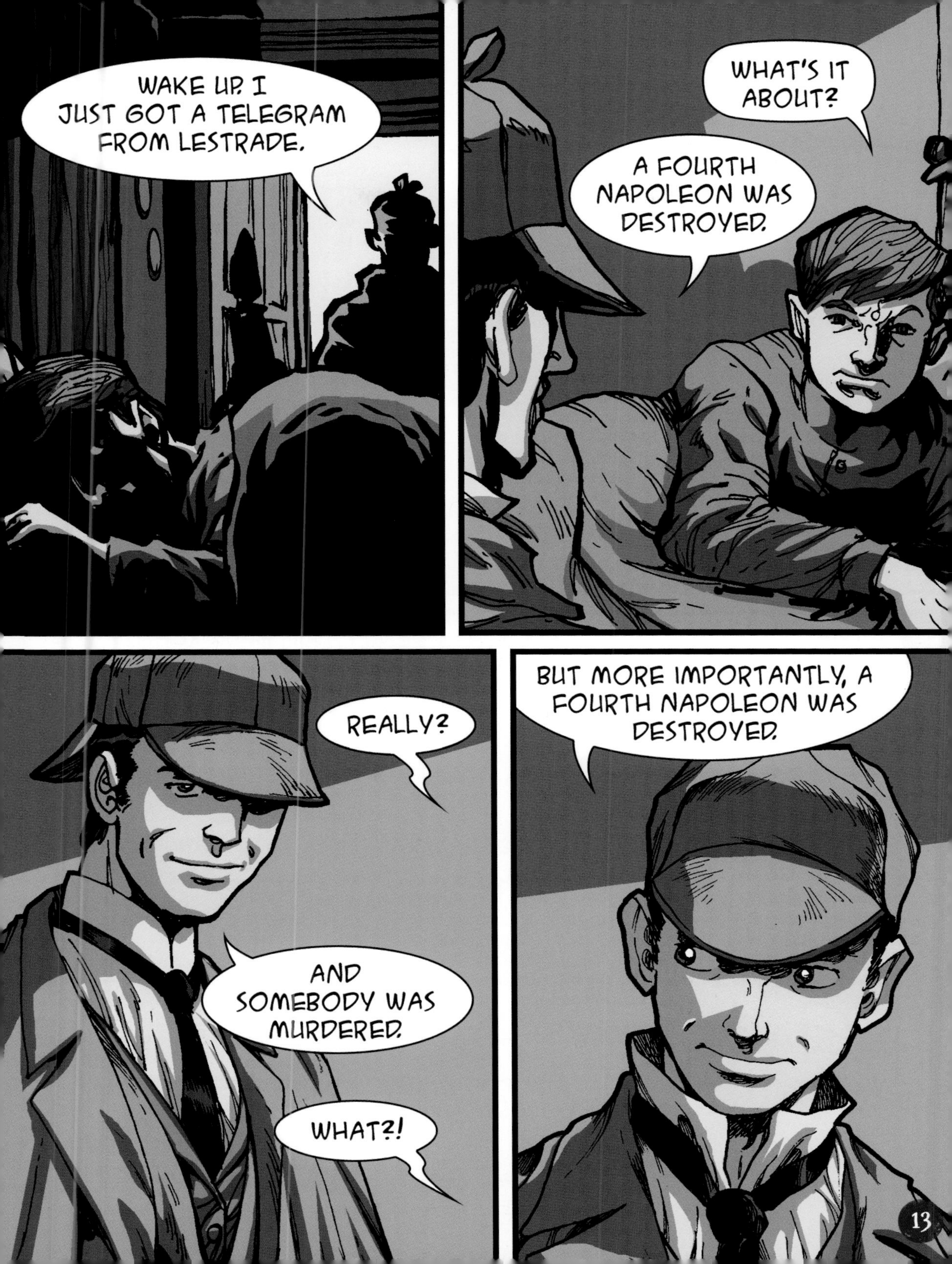
WAKE UP. I JUST GOT A TELEGRAM FROM LESTRADE.
WHAT'S IT ABOUT?
A FOURTH NAPOLEON WAS DESTROYED.
REALLY?
AND SOMEBODY WAS MURDERED.
WHAT?!
BUT MORE IMPORTANTLY, A FOURTH NAPOLEON WAS DESTROYED.

The home of Horace Harker...

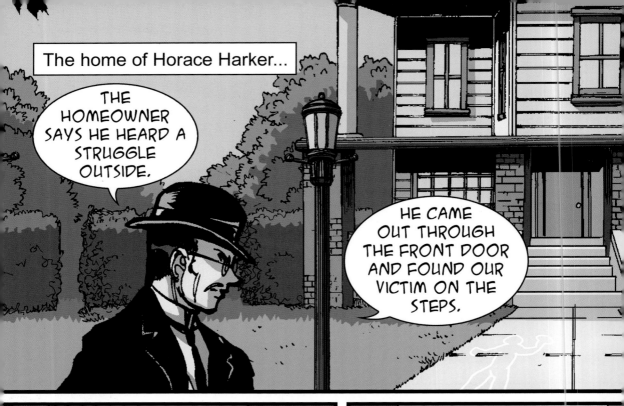

THE HOMEOWNER SAYS HE HEARD A STRUGGLE OUTSIDE.

HE CAME OUT THROUGH THE FRONT DOOR AND FOUND OUR VICTIM ON THE STEPS.

HE SAW A MAN RUN INTO THIS GARDEN, AND THEN HE HEARD A CRASH.

IT WAS THE NAPOLEON BUST BEING SMASHED.

PRECISELY.

DID HE PURCHASE THE BUST FROM MORSE HUDSON?

NO, HE BOUGHT IT FROM THE HARDING BROTHERS ABOUT FOUR MONTHS AGO.

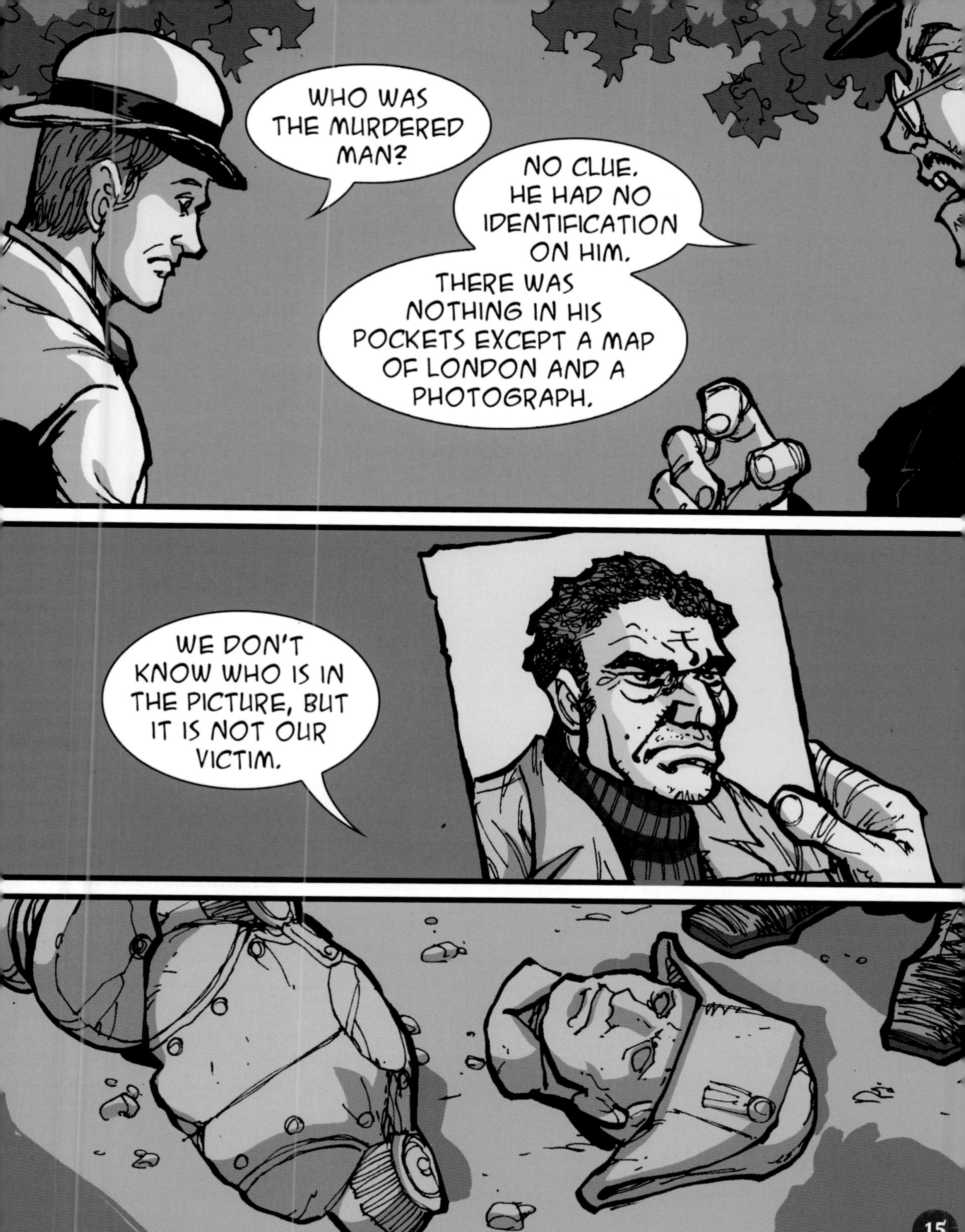
WHO WAS THE MURDERED MAN?
NO CLUE. HE HAD NO IDENTIFICATION ON HIM.
THERE WAS NOTHING IN HIS POCKETS EXCEPT A MAP OF LONDON AND A PHOTOGRAPH.
WE DON'T KNOW WHO IS IN THE PICTURE, BUT IT IS NOT OUR VICTIM.

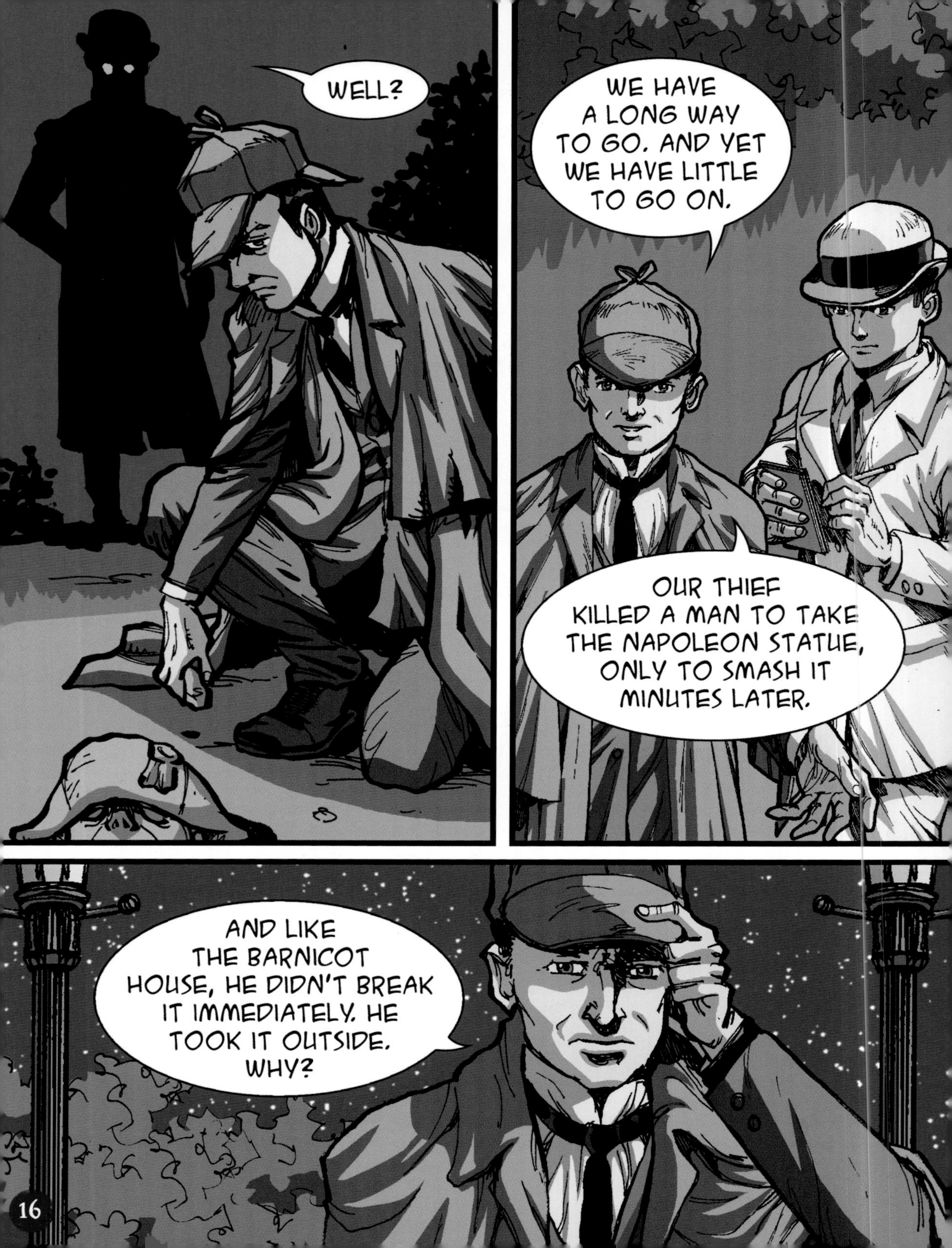
WELL?
WE HAVE A LONG WAY TO GO. AND YET WE HAVE LITTLE TO GO ON.
OUR THIEF KILLED A MAN TO TAKE THE NAPOLEON STATUE, ONLY TO SMASH IT MINUTES LATER.
AND LIKE THE BARNICOT HOUSE, HE DIDN'T BREAK IT IMMEDIATELY. HE TOOK IT OUTSIDE. WHY?

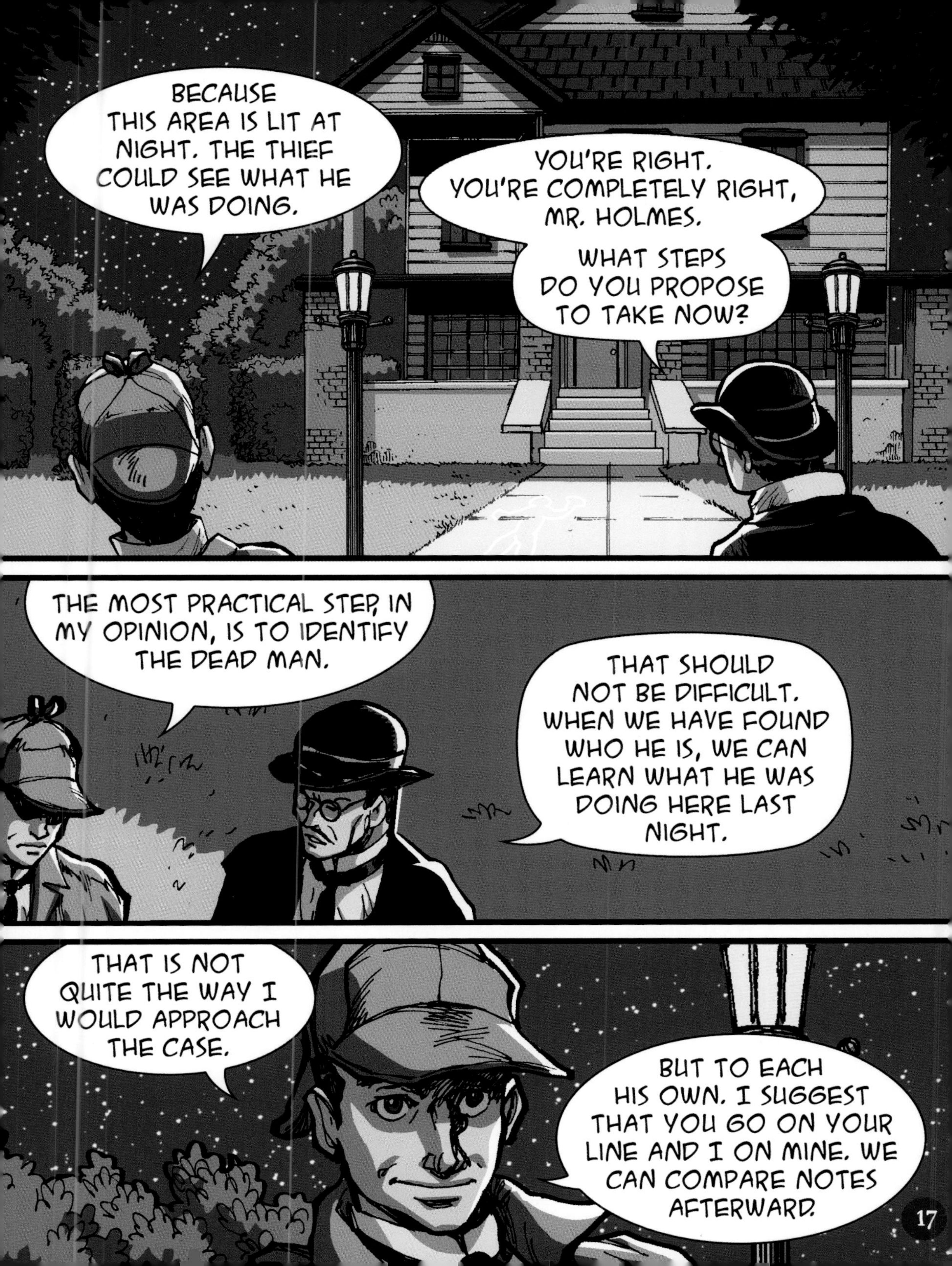
BECAUSE THIS AREA IS LIT AT NIGHT. THE THIEF COULD SEE WHAT HE WAS DOING.
YOU'RE RIGHT. YOU'RE COMPLETELY RIGHT, MR. HOLMES.
WHAT STEPS DO YOU PROPOSE TO TAKE NOW?
THE MOST PRACTICAL STEP, IN MY OPINION, IS TO IDENTIFY THE DEAD MAN.
THAT SHOULD NOT BE DIFFICULT. WHEN WE HAVE FOUND WHO HE IS, WE CAN LEARN WHAT HE WAS DOING HERE LAST NIGHT.
THAT IS NOT QUITE THE WAY I WOULD APPROACH THE CASE.
BUT TO EACH HIS OWN. I SUGGEST THAT YOU GO ON YOUR LINE AND I ON MINE. WE CAN COMPARE NOTES AFTERWARD.

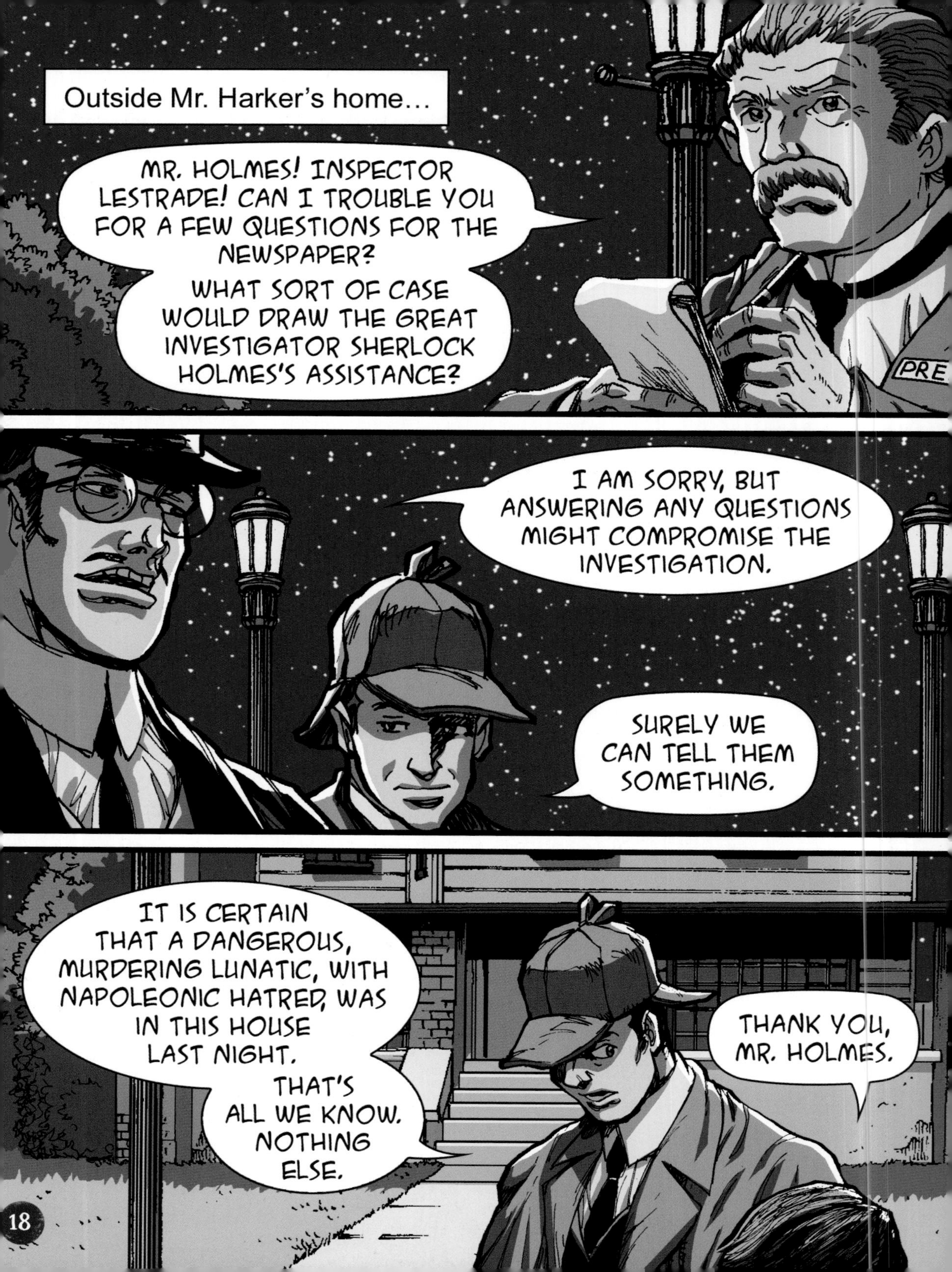
Outside Mr. Harker's home…
MR. HOLMES! INSPECTOR LESTRADE! CAN I TROUBLE YOU FOR A FEW QUESTIONS FOR THE NEWSPAPER?
WHAT SORT OF CASE WOULD DRAW THE GREAT INVESTIGATOR SHERLOCK HOLMES'S ASSISTANCE?
PRE
I AM SORRY, BUT ANSWERING ANY QUESTIONS MIGHT COMPROMISE THE INVESTIGATION.
SURELY WE CAN TELL THEM SOMETHING.
IT IS CERTAIN THAT A DANGEROUS, MURDERING LUNATIC, WITH NAPOLEONIC HATRED, WAS IN THIS HOUSE LAST NIGHT.
THAT'S ALL WE KNOW. NOTHING ELSE.
THANK YOU, MR. HOLMES.

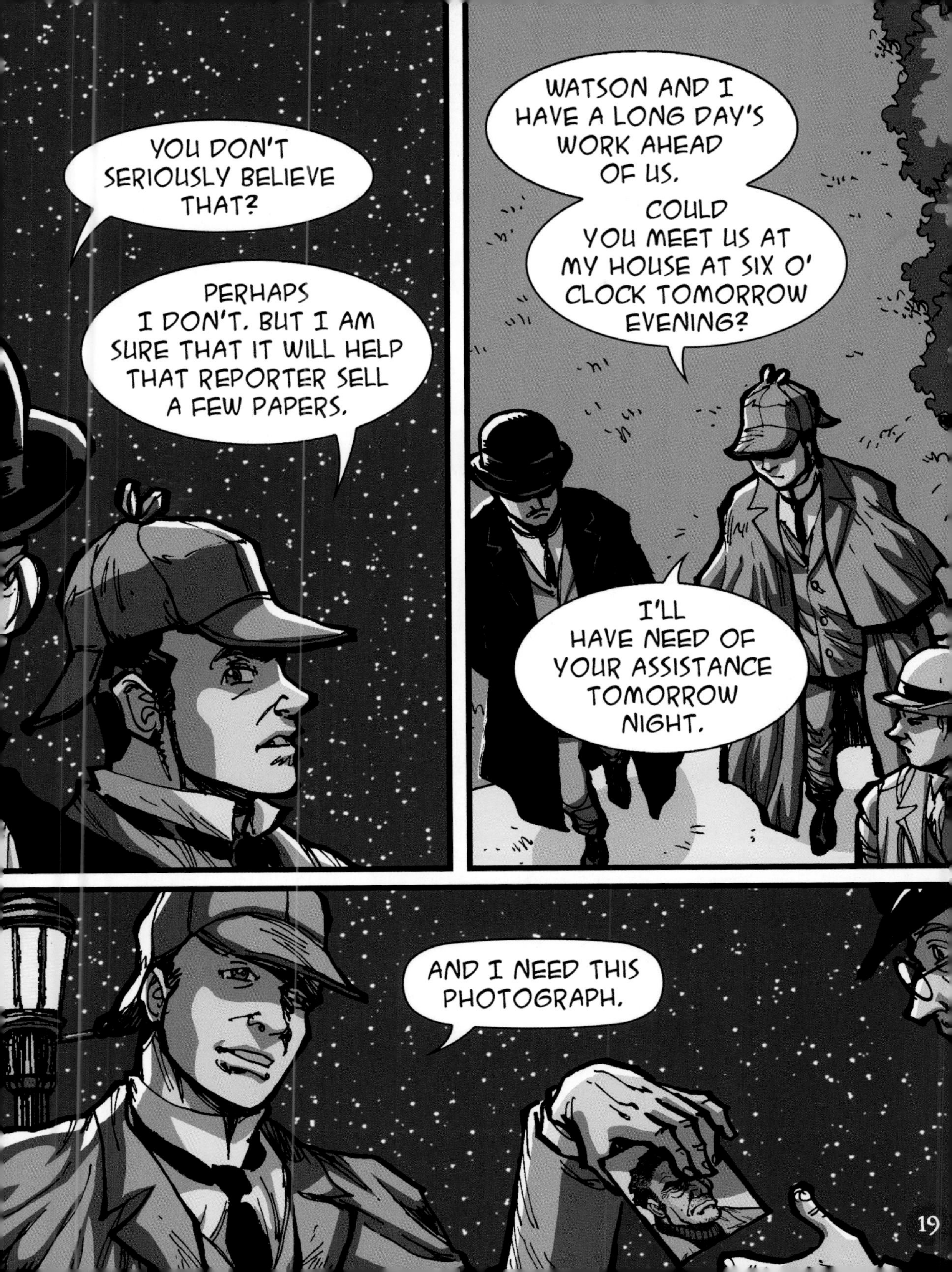
YOU DON'T SERIOUSLY BELIEVE THAT?
PERHAPS I DON'T. BUT I AM SURE THAT IT WILL HELP THAT REPORTER SELL A FEW PAPERS.
WATSON AND I HAVE A LONG DAY'S WORK AHEAD OF US.
COULD YOU MEET US AT MY HOUSE AT SIX O' CLOCK TOMORROW EVENING?
I'LL HAVE NEED OF YOUR ASSISTANCE TOMORROW NIGHT.
AND I NEED THIS PHOTOGRAPH.

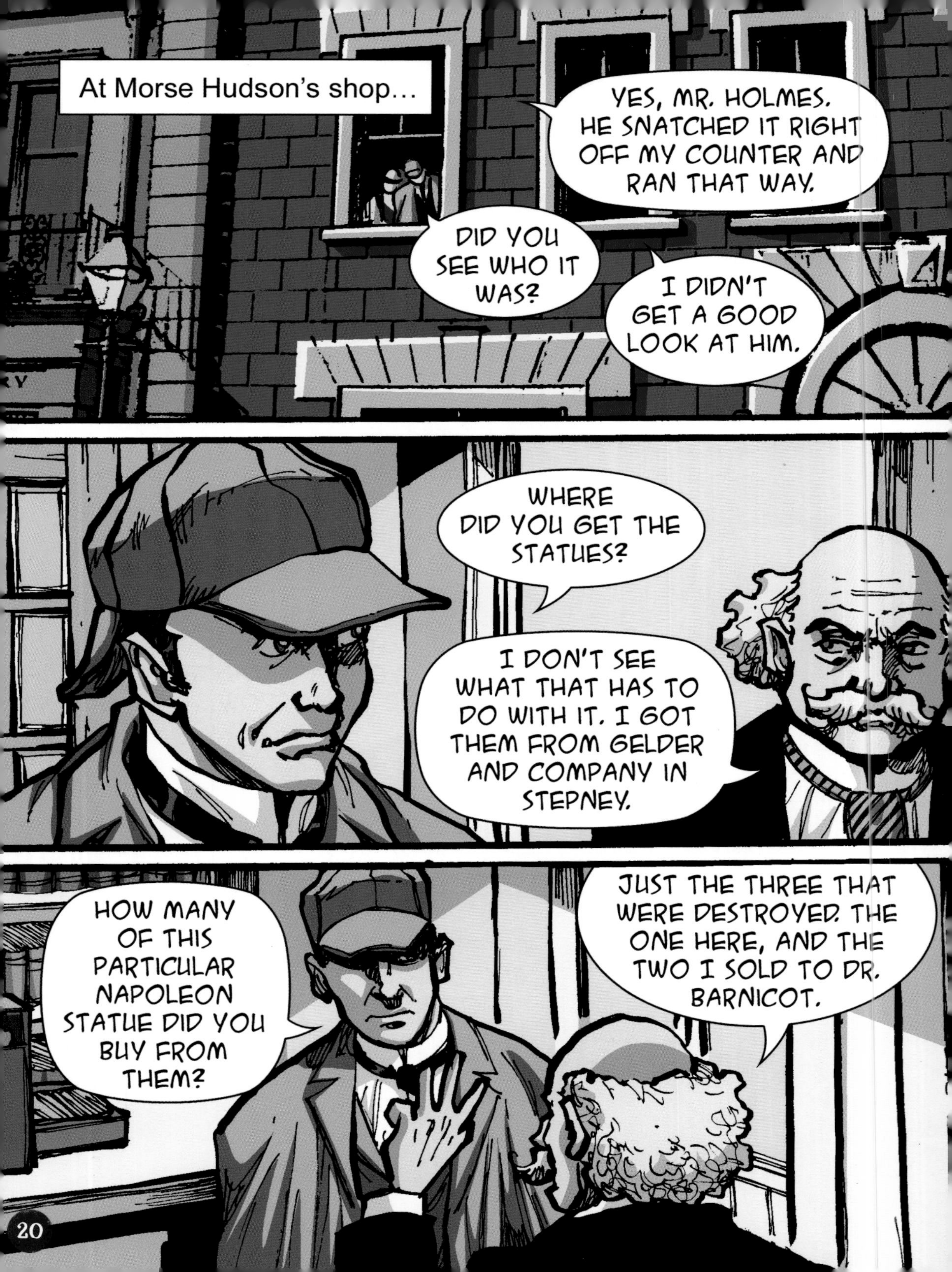

At Morse Hudson's shop…
YES, MR. HOLMES. HE SNATCHED IT RIGHT OFF MY COUNTER AND RAN THAT WAY.
DID YOU SEE WHO IT WAS?
I DIDN'T GET A GOOD LOOK AT HIM.
WHERE DID YOU GET THE STATUES?
I DON'T SEE WHAT THAT HAS TO DO WITH IT. I GOT THEM FROM GELDER AND COMPANY IN STEPNEY.
HOW MANY OF THIS PARTICULAR NAPOLEON STATUE DID YOU BUY FROM THEM?
JUST THE THREE THAT WERE DESTROYED. THE ONE HERE, AND THE TWO I SOLD TO DR. BARNICOT.

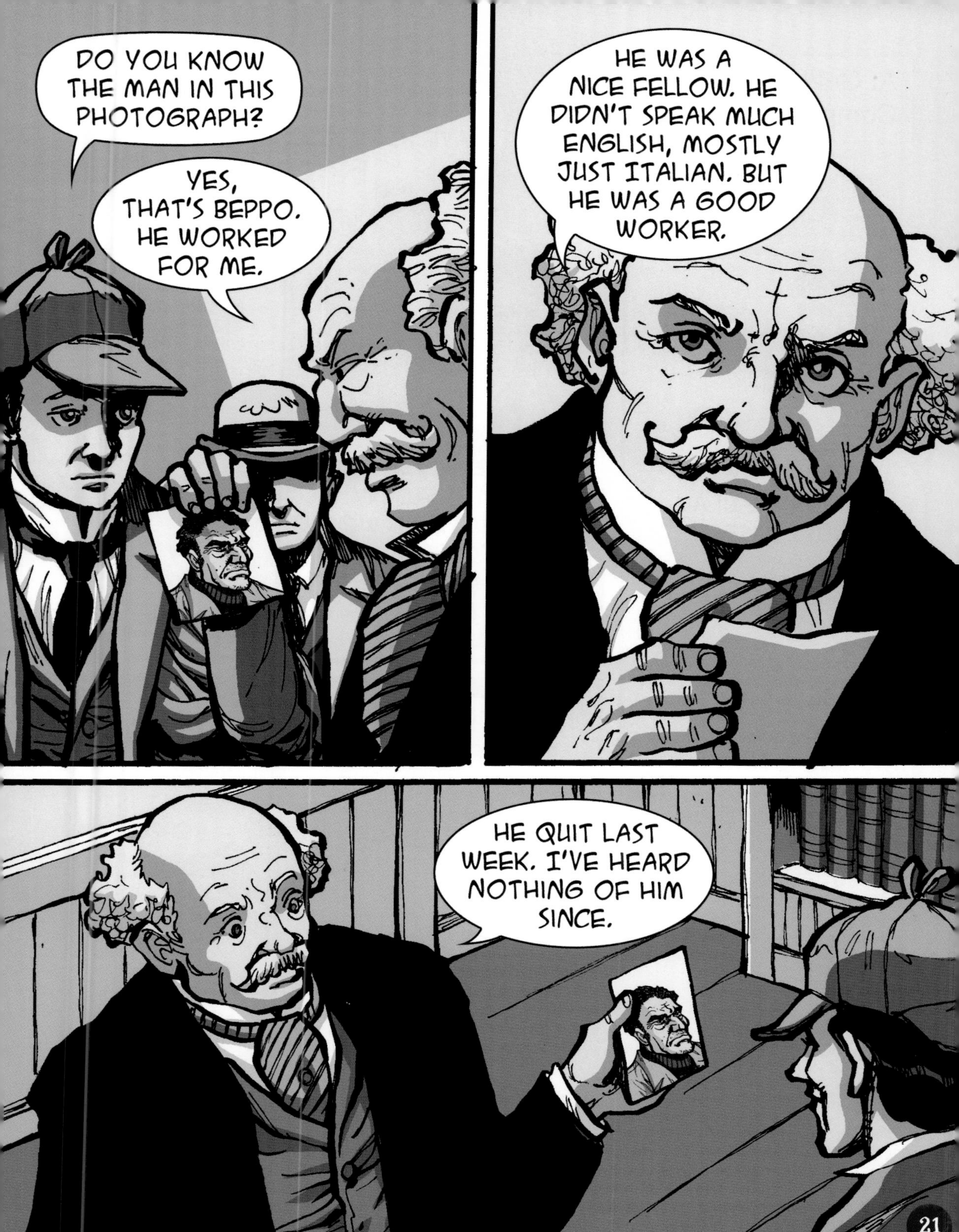
DO YOU KNOW THE MAN IN THIS PHOTOGRAPH?
YES, THAT'S BEPPO. HE WORKED FOR ME.
HE WAS A NICE FELLOW. HE DIDN'T SPEAK MUCH ENGLISH, MOSTLY JUST ITALIAN. BUT HE WAS A GOOD WORKER.
HE QUIT LAST WEEK. I'VE HEARD NOTHING OF HIM SINCE.

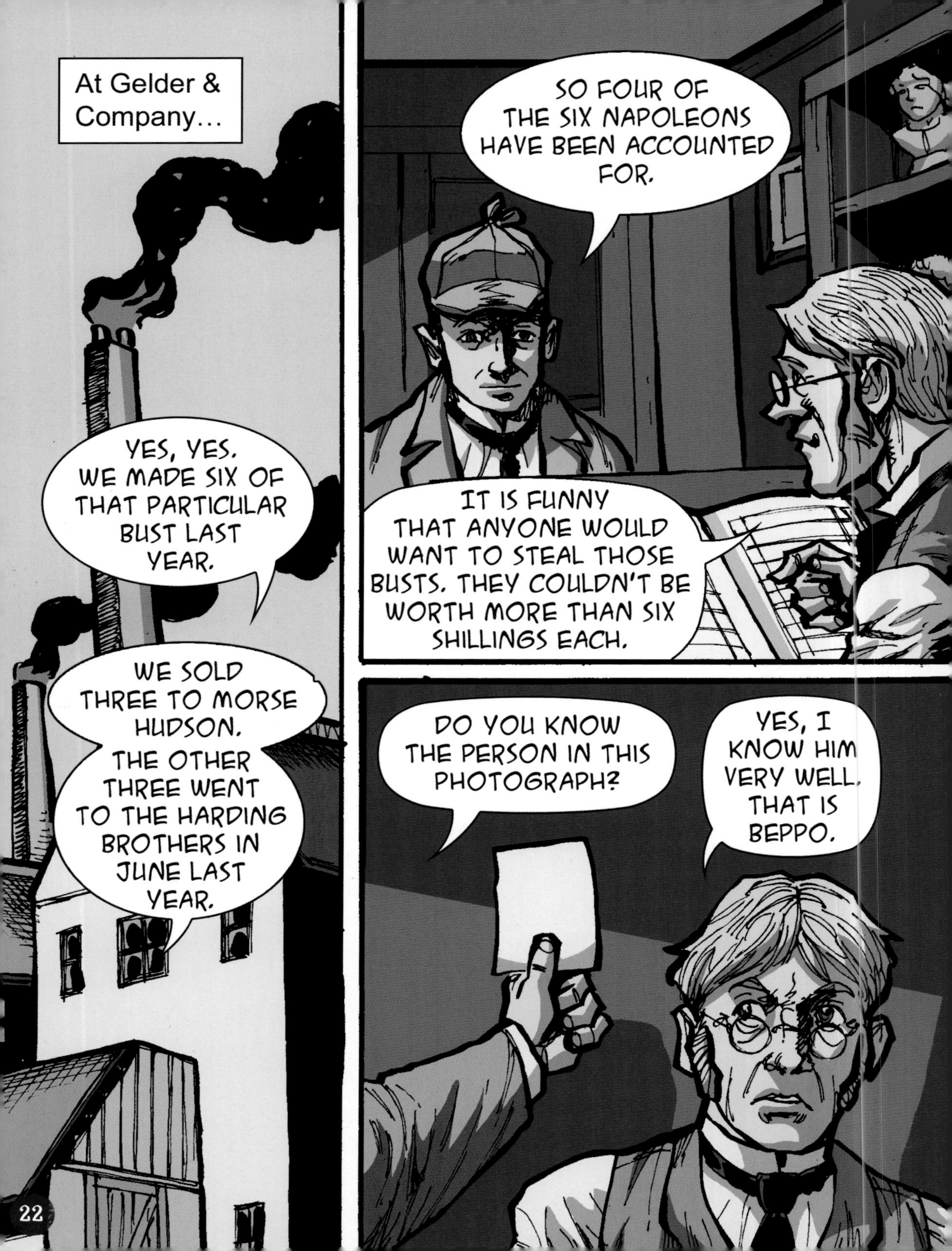

At Gelder & Company…
YES, YES. WE MADE SIX OF THAT PARTICULAR BUST LAST YEAR.
WE SOLD THREE TO MORSE HUDSON.
THE OTHER THREE WENT TO THE HARDING BROTHERS IN JUNE LAST YEAR.
SO FOUR OF THE SIX NAPOLEONS HAVE BEEN ACCOUNTED FOR.
IT IS FUNNY THAT ANYONE WOULD WANT TO STEAL THOSE BUSTS. THEY COULDN'T BE WORTH MORE THAN SIX SHILLINGS EACH.
DO YOU KNOW THE PERSON IN THIS PHOTOGRAPH?
YES, I KNOW HIM VERY WELL. THAT IS BEPPO.

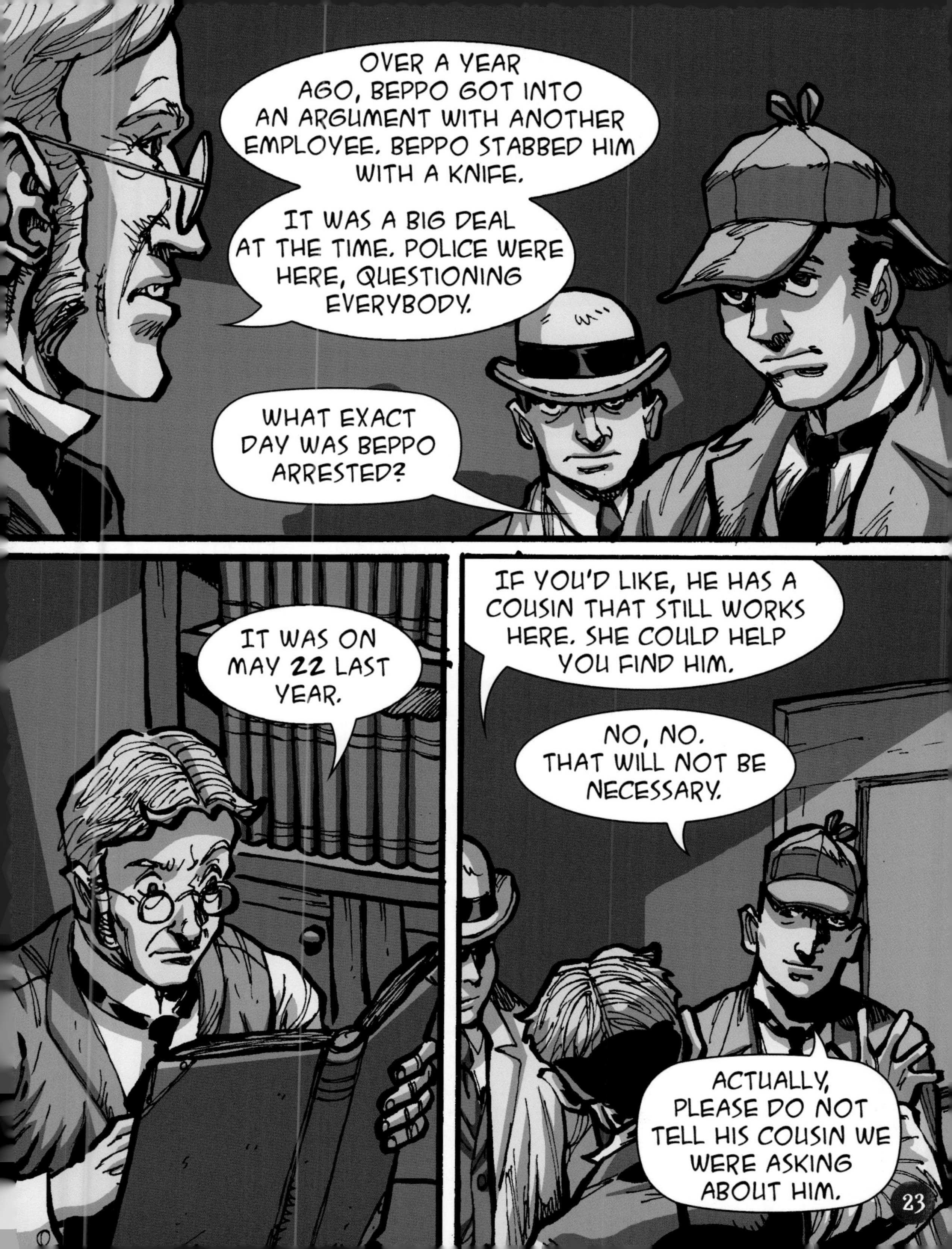
OVER A YEAR AGO, BEPPO GOT INTO AN ARGUMENT WITH ANOTHER EMPLOYEE. BEPPO STABBED HIM WITH A KNIFE.
IT WAS A BIG DEAL AT THE TIME. POLICE WERE HERE, QUESTIONING EVERYBODY.
WHAT EXACT DAY WAS BEPPO ARRESTED?
IT WAS ON MAY 22 LAST YEAR.
IF YOU'D LIKE, HE HAS A COUSIN THAT STILL WORKS HERE. SHE COULD HELP YOU FIND HIM.
NO, NO. THAT WILL NOT BE NECESSARY.
ACTUALLY, PLEASE DO NOT TELL HIS COUSIN WE WERE ASKING ABOUT HIM.

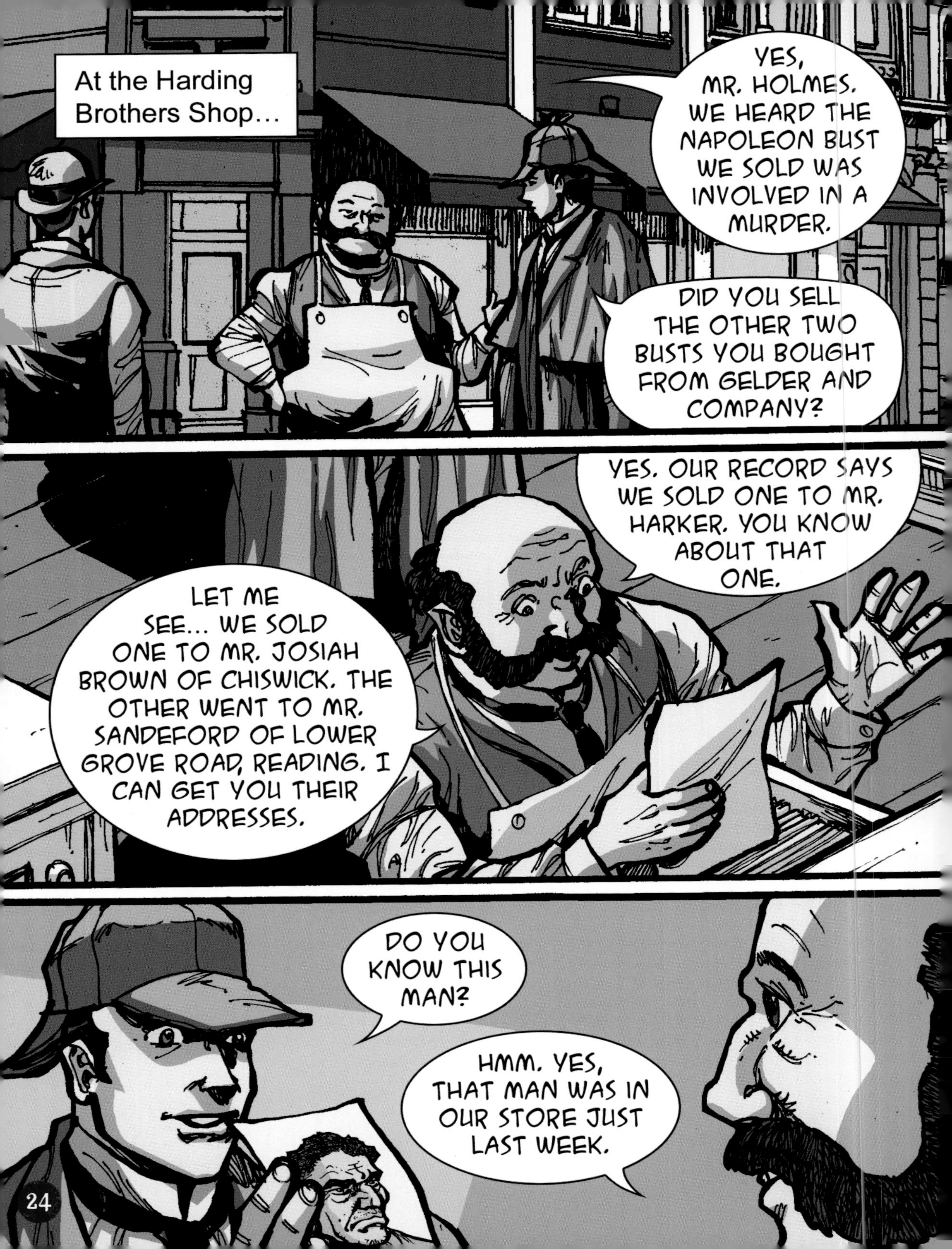

At the Harding Brothers Shop…
YES, MR. HOLMES. WE HEARD THE NAPOLEON BUST WE SOLD WAS INVOLVED IN A MURDER.
DID YOU SELL THE OTHER TWO BUSTS YOU BOUGHT FROM GELDER AND COMPANY?
YES. OUR RECORD SAYS WE SOLD ONE TO MR. HARKER. YOU KNOW ABOUT THAT ONE.
LET ME SEE… WE SOLD ONE TO MR. JOSIAH BROWN OF CHISWICK. THE OTHER WENT TO MR. SANDEFORD OF LOWER GROVE ROAD, READING. I CAN GET YOU THEIR ADDRESSES.
DO YOU KNOW THIS MAN?
HMM. YES, THAT MAN WAS IN OUR STORE JUST LAST WEEK.

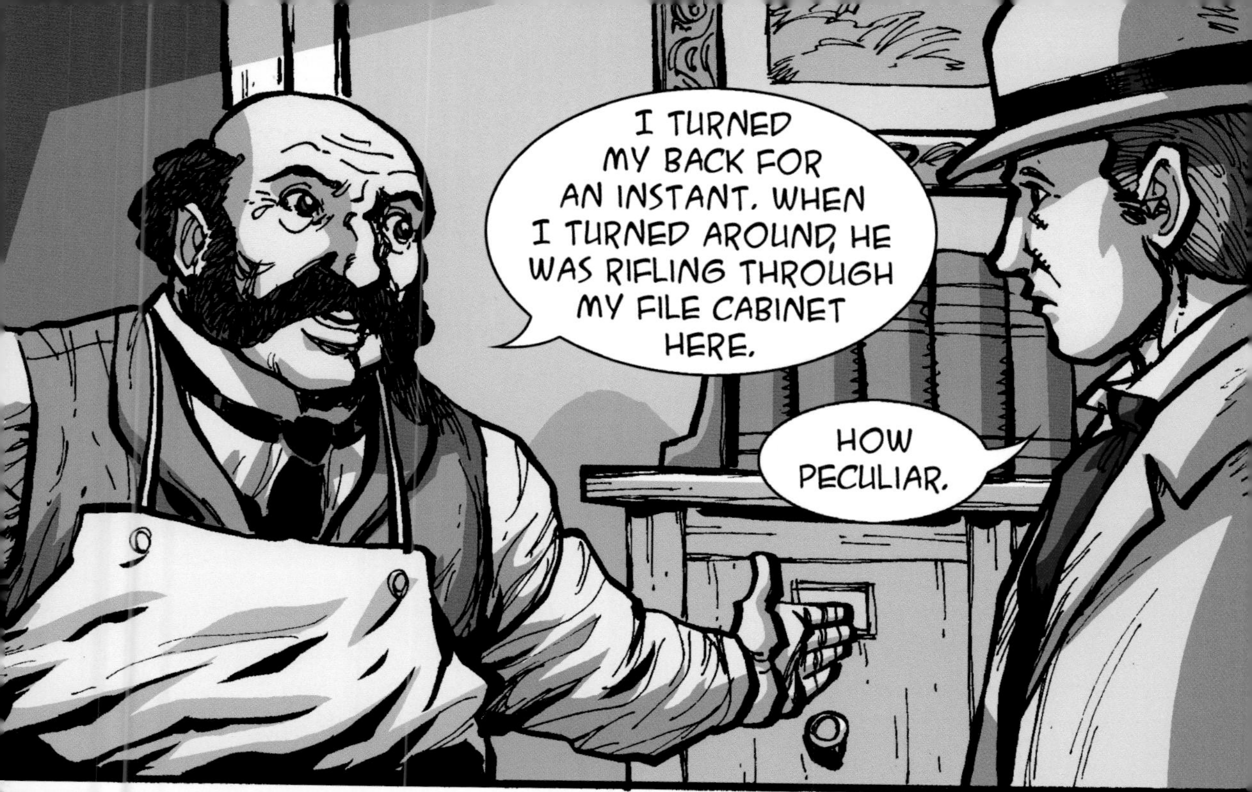
I TURNED MY BACK FOR AN INSTANT. WHEN I TURNED AROUND, HE WAS RIFLING THROUGH MY FILE CABINET HERE.
HOW PECULIAR.

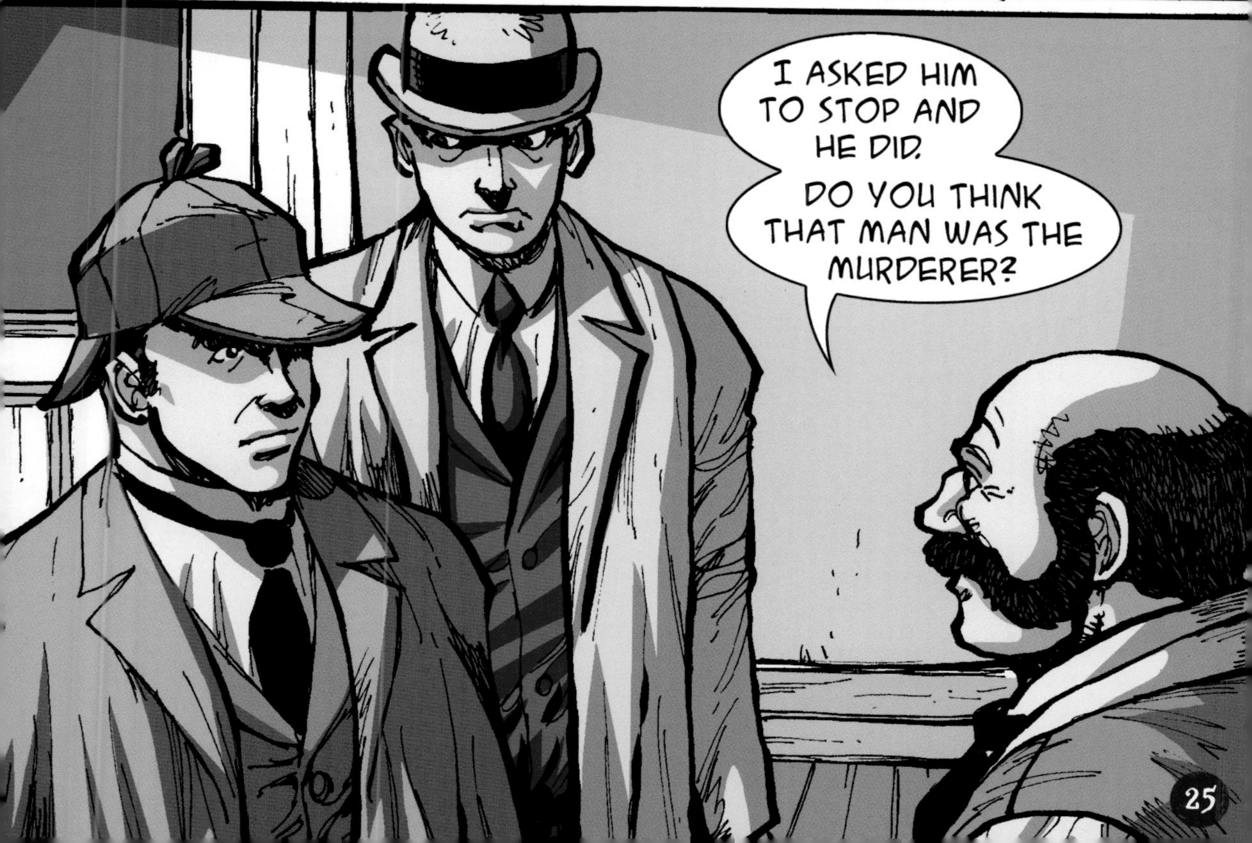
I ASKED HIM TO STOP AND HE DID.
DO YOU THINK THAT MAN WAS THE MURDERER?

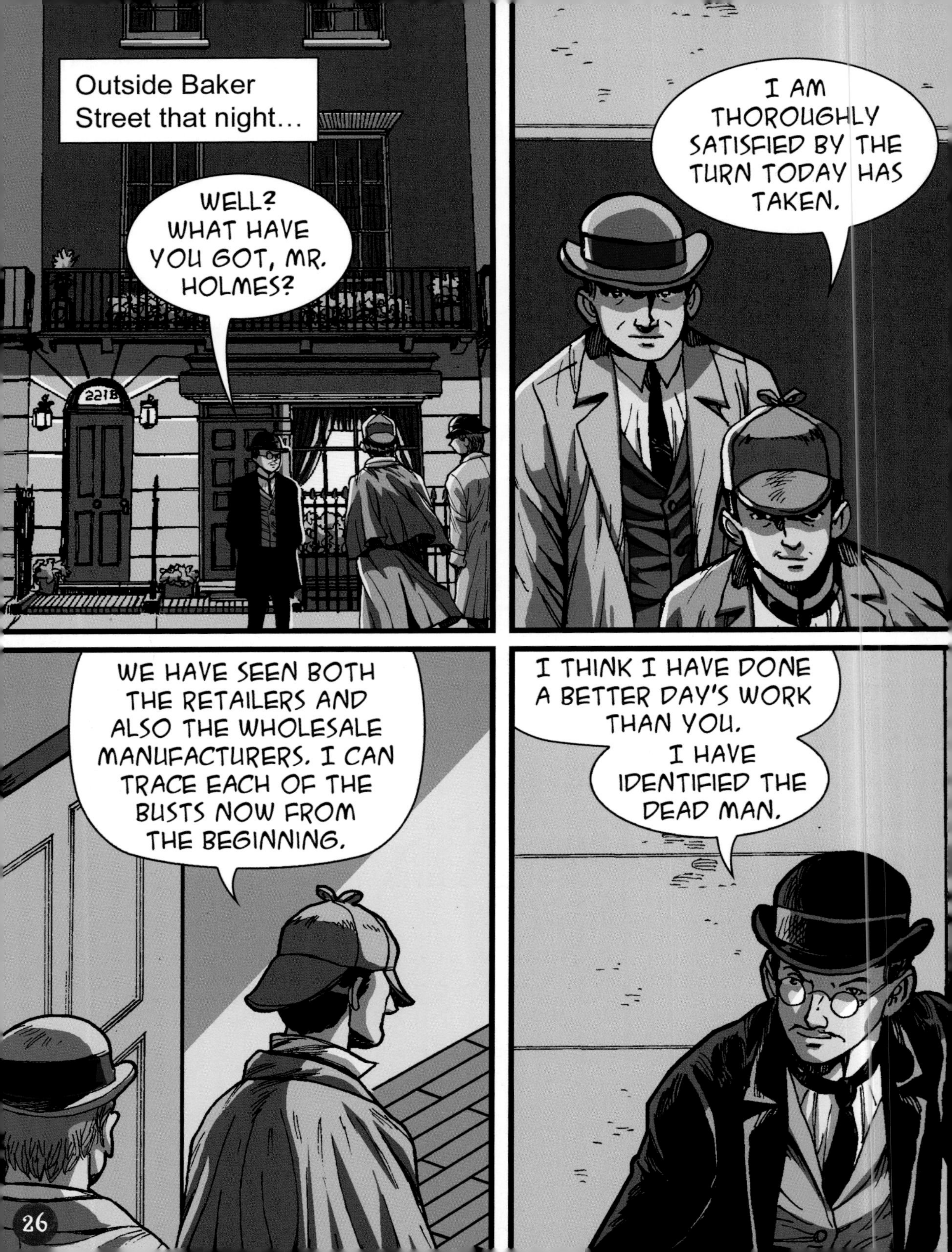
Outside Baker Street that night…
2218
WELL? WHAT HAVE YOU GOT, MR. HOLMES?
I AM THOROUGHLY SATISFIED BY THE TURN TODAY HAS TAKEN.
WE HAVE SEEN BOTH THE RETAILERS AND ALSO THE WHOLESALE MANUFACTURERS. I CAN TRACE EACH OF THE BUSTS NOW FROM THE BEGINNING.
I THINK I HAVE DONE A BETTER DAY'S WORK THAN YOU.
I HAVE IDENTIFIED THE DEAD MAN.

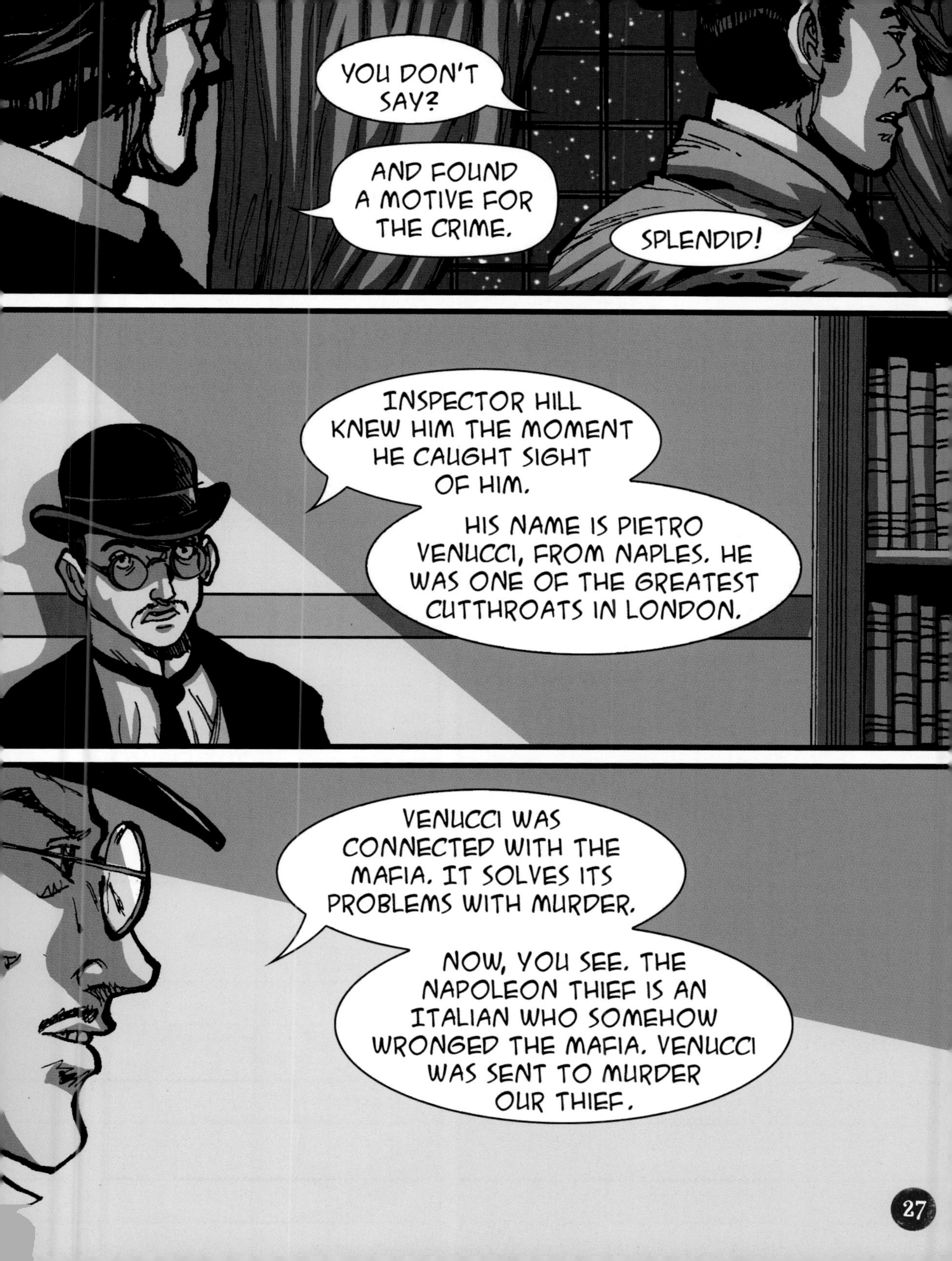
YOU DON'T SAY?
AND FOUND A MOTIVE FOR THE CRIME.
SPLENDID!
INSPECTOR HILL KNEW HIM THE MOMENT HE CAUGHT SIGHT OF HIM.
HIS NAME IS PIETRO VENUCCI, FROM NAPLES. HE WAS ONE OF THE GREATEST CUTTHROATS IN LONDON.
VENUCCI WAS CONNECTED WITH THE MAFIA. IT SOLVES ITS PROBLEMS WITH MURDER.
NOW, YOU SEE. THE NAPOLEON THIEF IS AN ITALIAN WHO SOMEHOW WRONGED THE MAFIA. VENUCCI WAS SENT TO MURDER OUR THIEF.

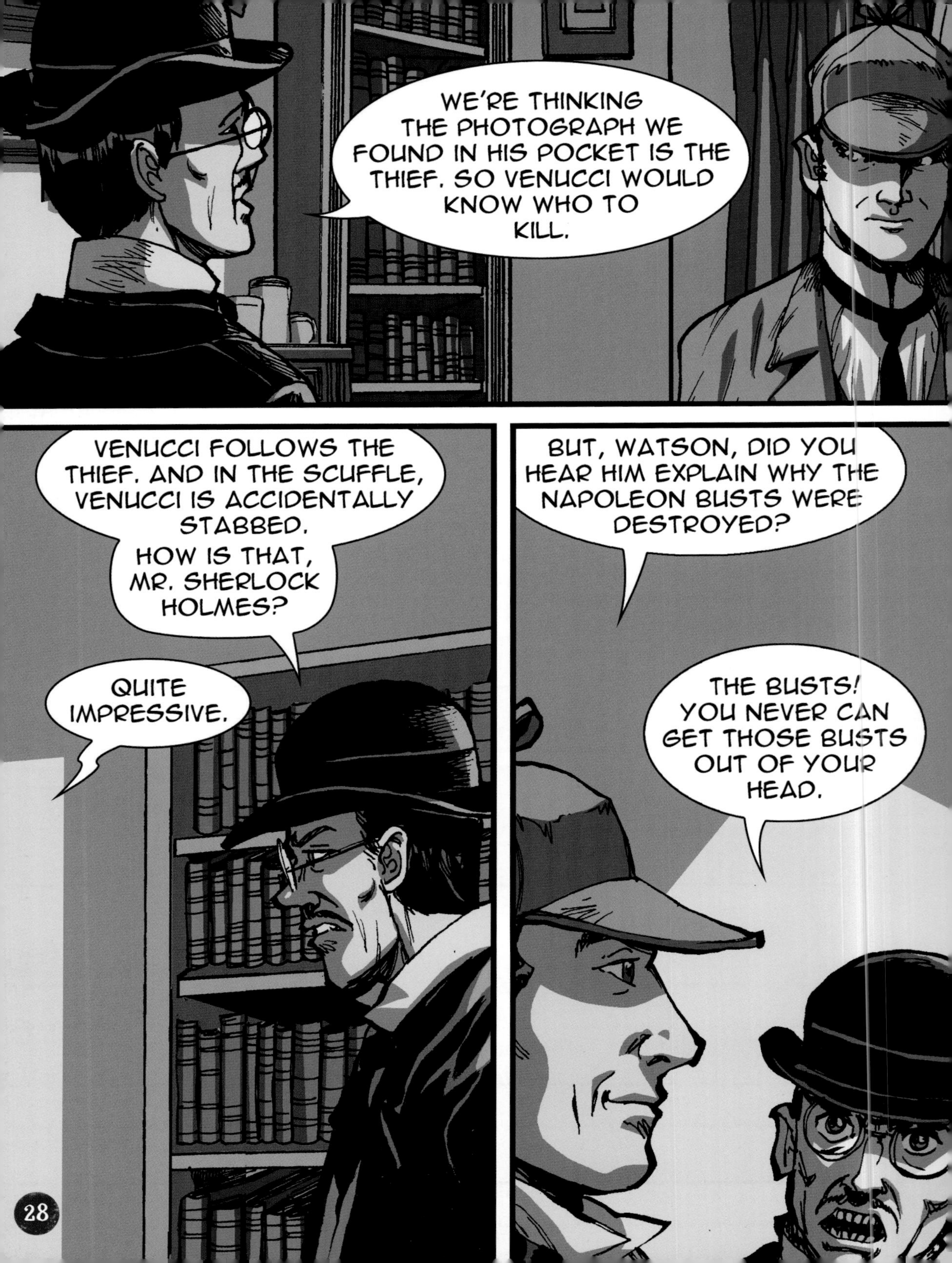
WE'RE THINKING THE PHOTOGRAPH WE FOUND IN HIS POCKET IS THE THIEF. SO VENUCCI WOULD KNOW WHO TO KILL.
VENUCCI FOLLOWS THE THIEF. AND IN THE SCUFFLE, VENUCCI IS ACCIDENTALLY STABBED. HOW IS THAT, MR. SHERLOCK HOLMES?
QUITE IMPRESSIVE.
BUT, WATSON, DID YOU HEAR HIM EXPLAIN WHY THE NAPOLEON BUSTS WERE DESTROYED?
THE BUSTS! YOU NEVER CAN GET THOSE BUSTS OUT OF YOUR HEAD.

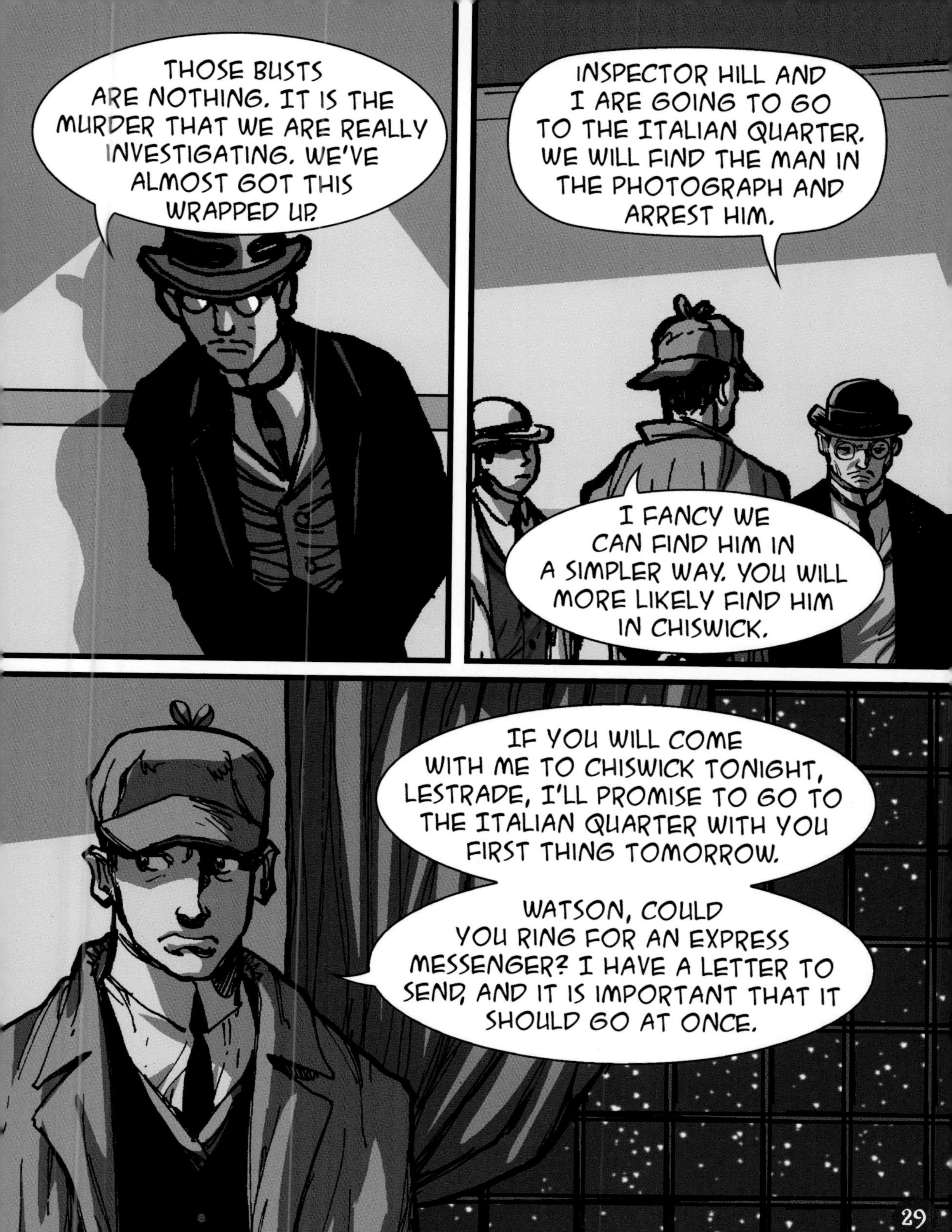
THOSE BUSTS ARE NOTHING. IT IS THE MURDER THAT WE ARE REALLY INVESTIGATING. WE'VE ALMOST GOT THIS WRAPPED UP.
INSPECTOR HILL AND I ARE GOING TO GO TO THE ITALIAN QUARTER. WE WILL FIND THE MAN IN THE PHOTOGRAPH AND ARREST HIM.
I FANCY WE CAN FIND HIM IN A SIMPLER WAY. YOU WILL MORE LIKELY FIND HIM IN CHISWICK.
IF YOU WILL COME WITH ME TO CHISWICK TONIGHT, LESTRADE, I'LL PROMISE TO GO TO THE ITALIAN QUARTER WITH YOU FIRST THING TOMORROW.
WATSON, COULD YOU RING FOR AN EXPRESS MESSENGER? I HAVE A LETTER TO SEND, AND IT IS IMPORTANT THAT IT SHOULD GO AT ONCE.

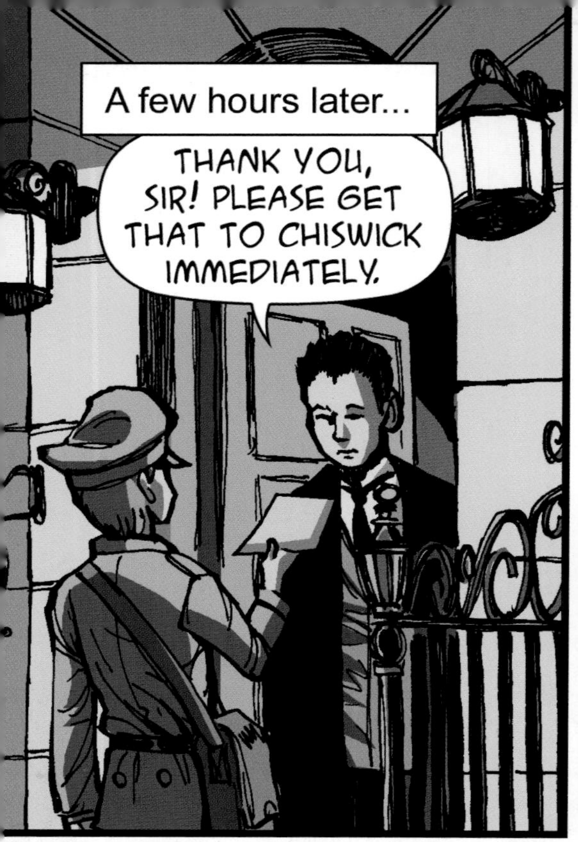
A few hours later...
THANK YOU, SIR! PLEASE GET THAT TO CHISWICK IMMEDIATELY.

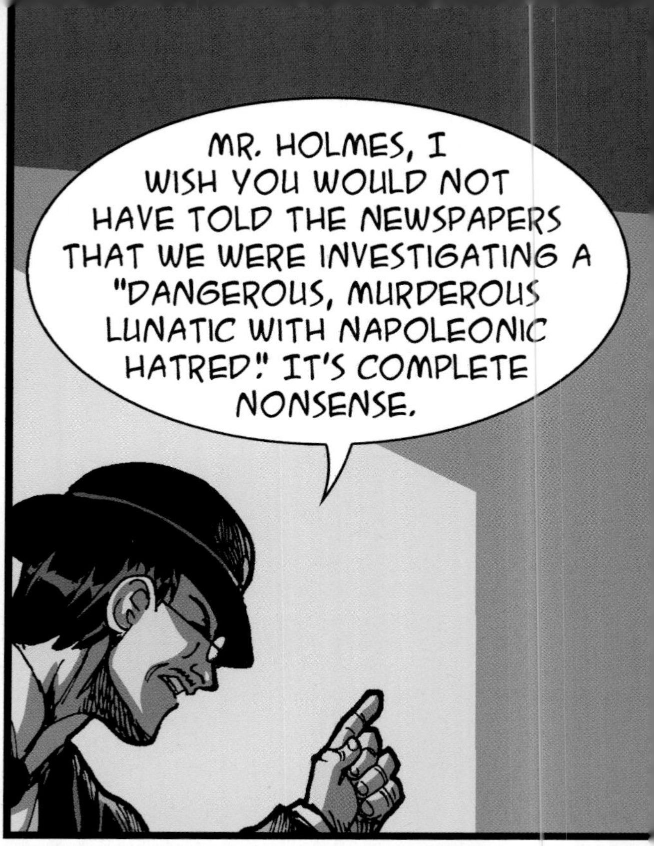
MR. HOLMES, I WISH YOU WOULD NOT HAVE TOLD THE NEWSPAPERS THAT WE WERE INVESTIGATING A "DANGEROUS, MURDEROUS LUNATIC WITH NAPOLEONIC HATRED." IT'S COMPLETE NONSENSE.

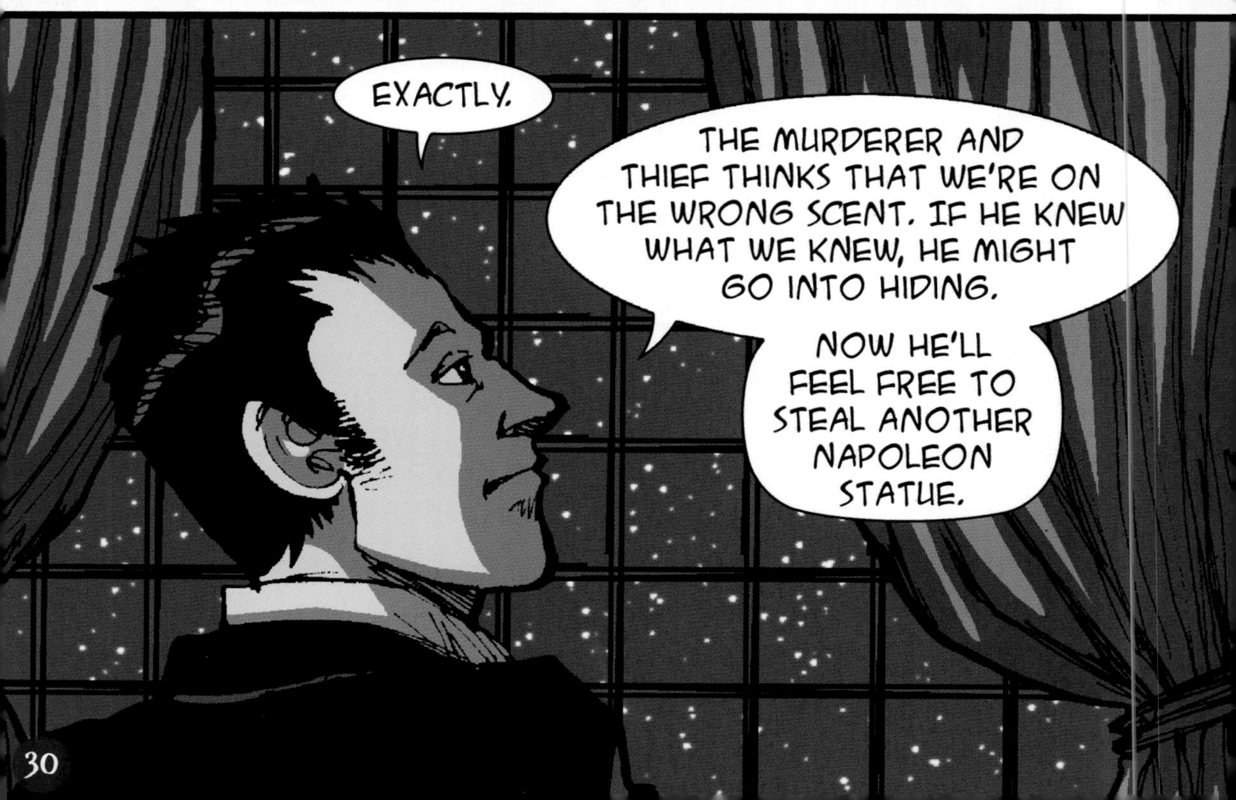
EXACTLY.
THE MURDERER AND THIEF THINKS THAT WE'RE ON THE WRONG SCENT. IF HE KNEW WHAT WE KNEW, HE MIGHT GO INTO HIDING.
NOW HE'LL FEEL FREE TO STEAL ANOTHER NAPOLEON STATUE.

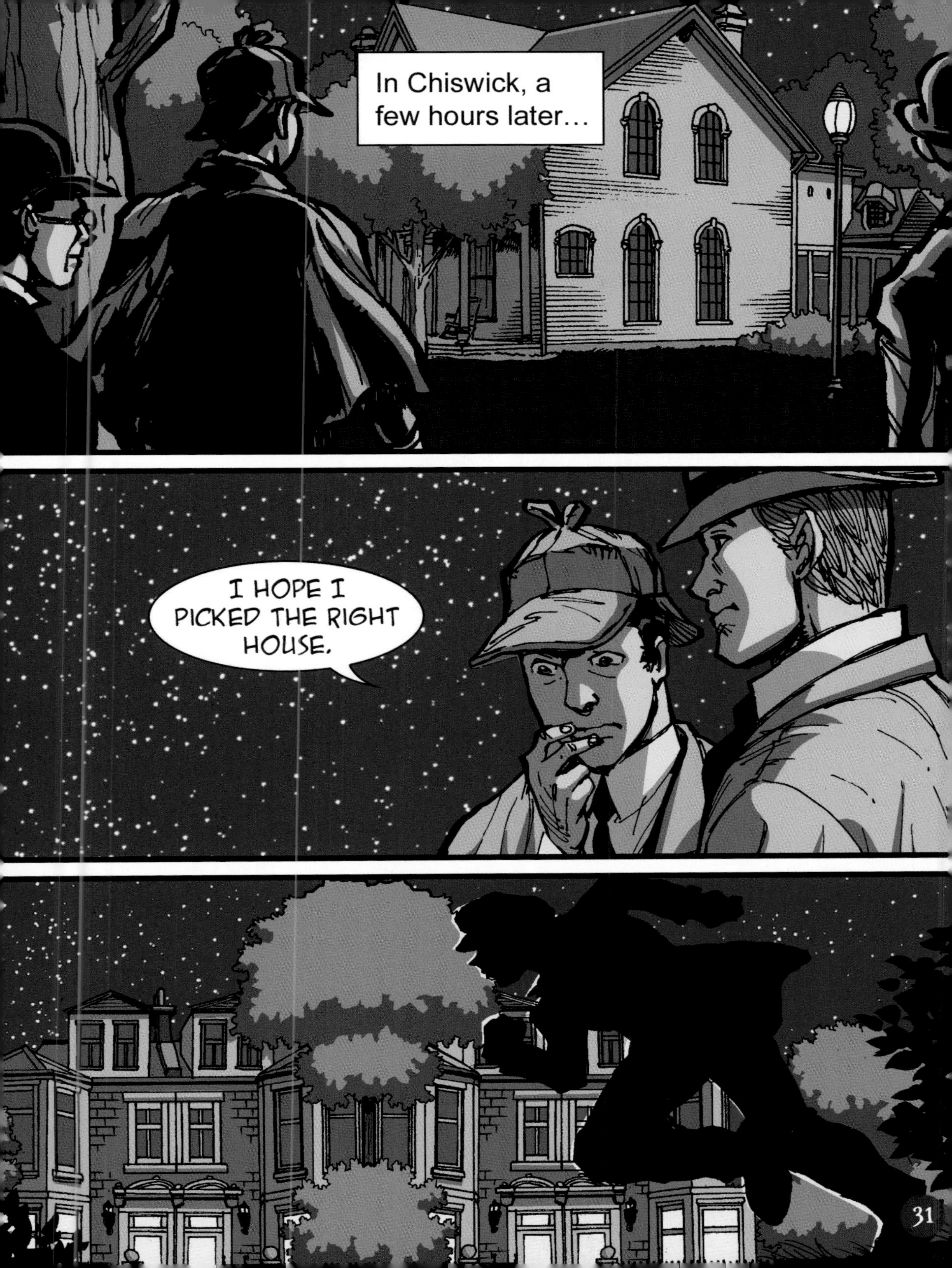
In Chiswick, a few hours later…
I HOPE I PICKED THE RIGHT HOUSE.

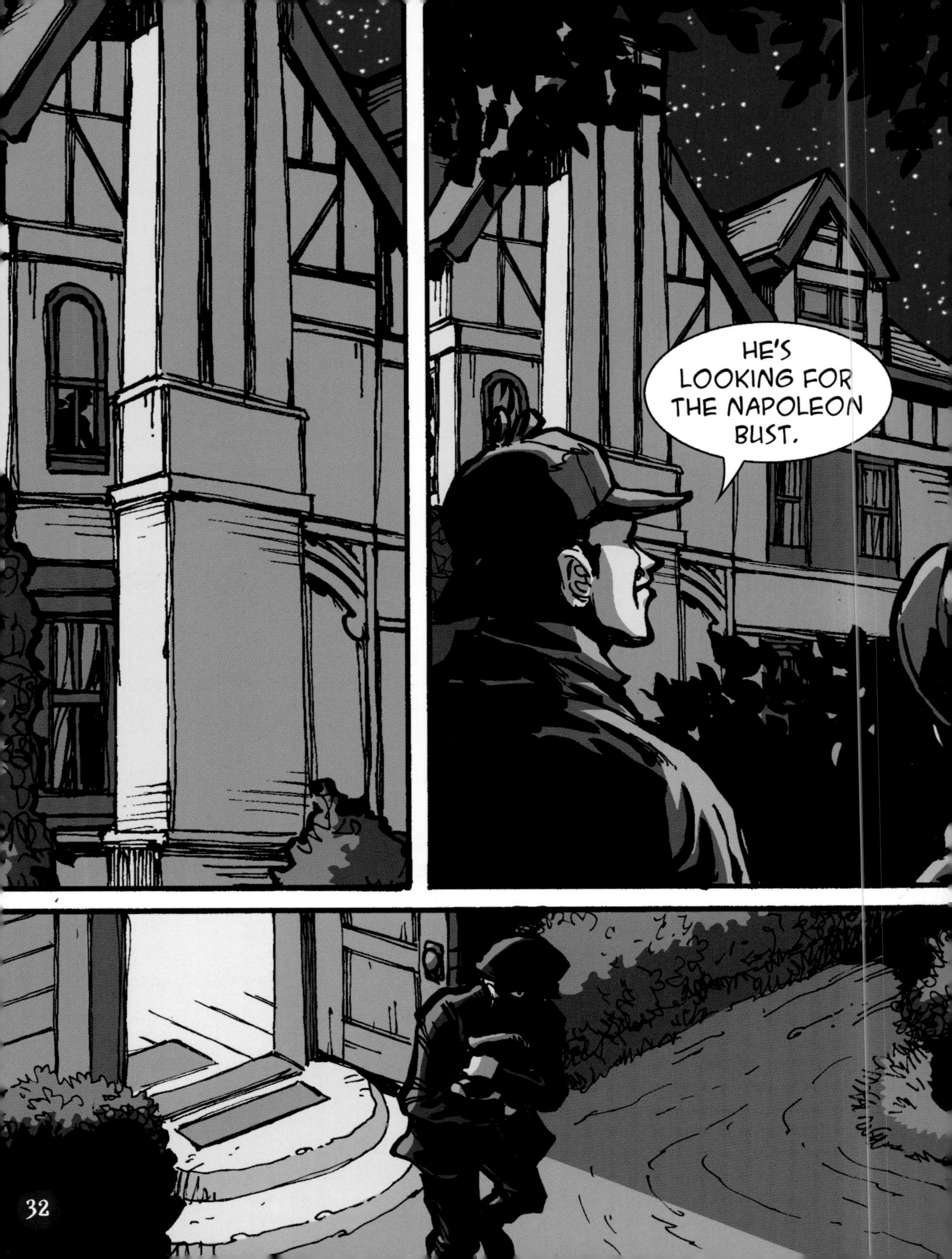
HE'S LOOKING FOR THE NAPOLEON BUST.

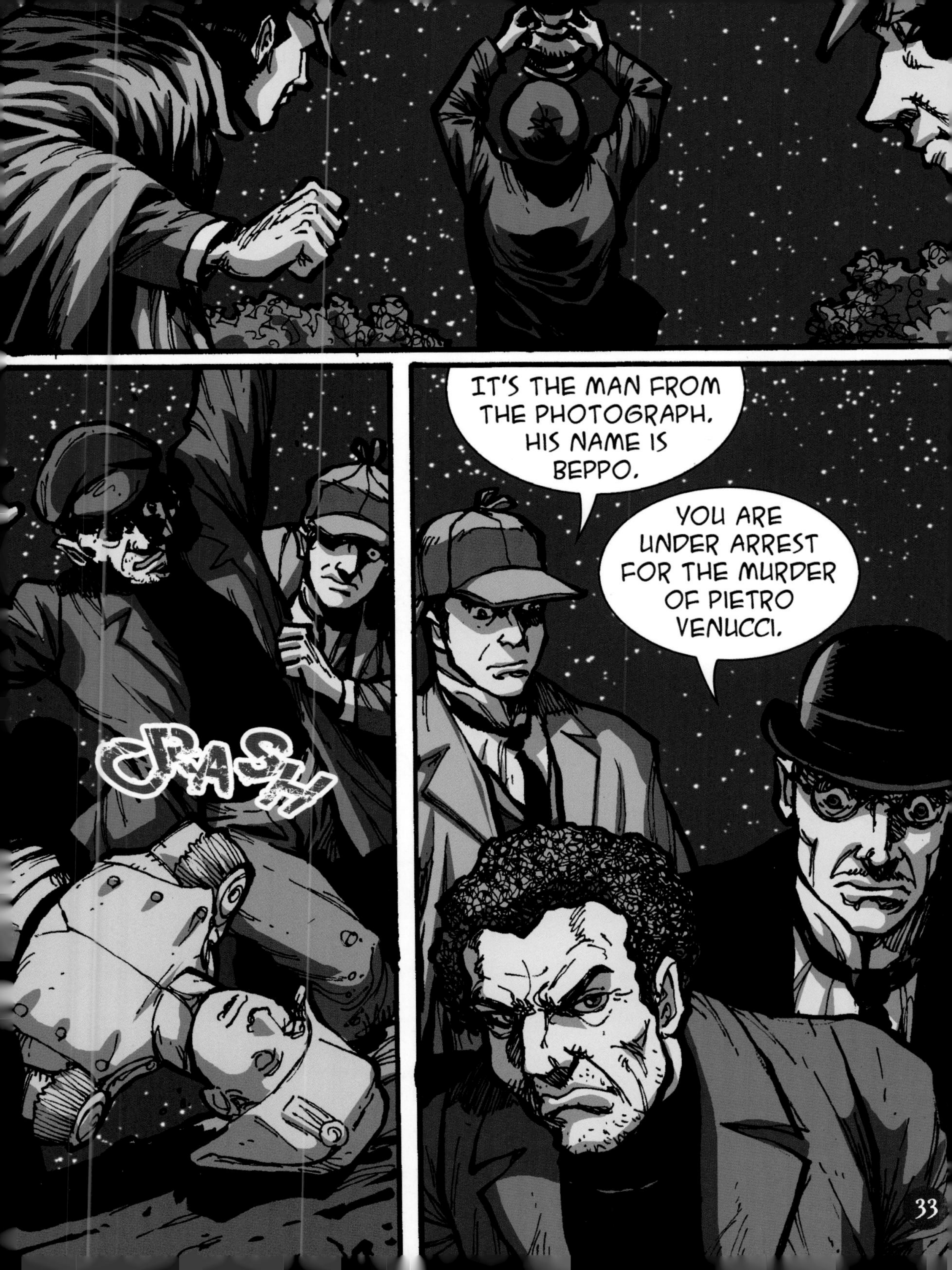
CRASH
IT'S THE MAN FROM THE PHOTOGRAPH. HIS NAME IS BEPPO.
YOU ARE UNDER ARREST FOR THE MURDER OF PIETRO VENUCCI.

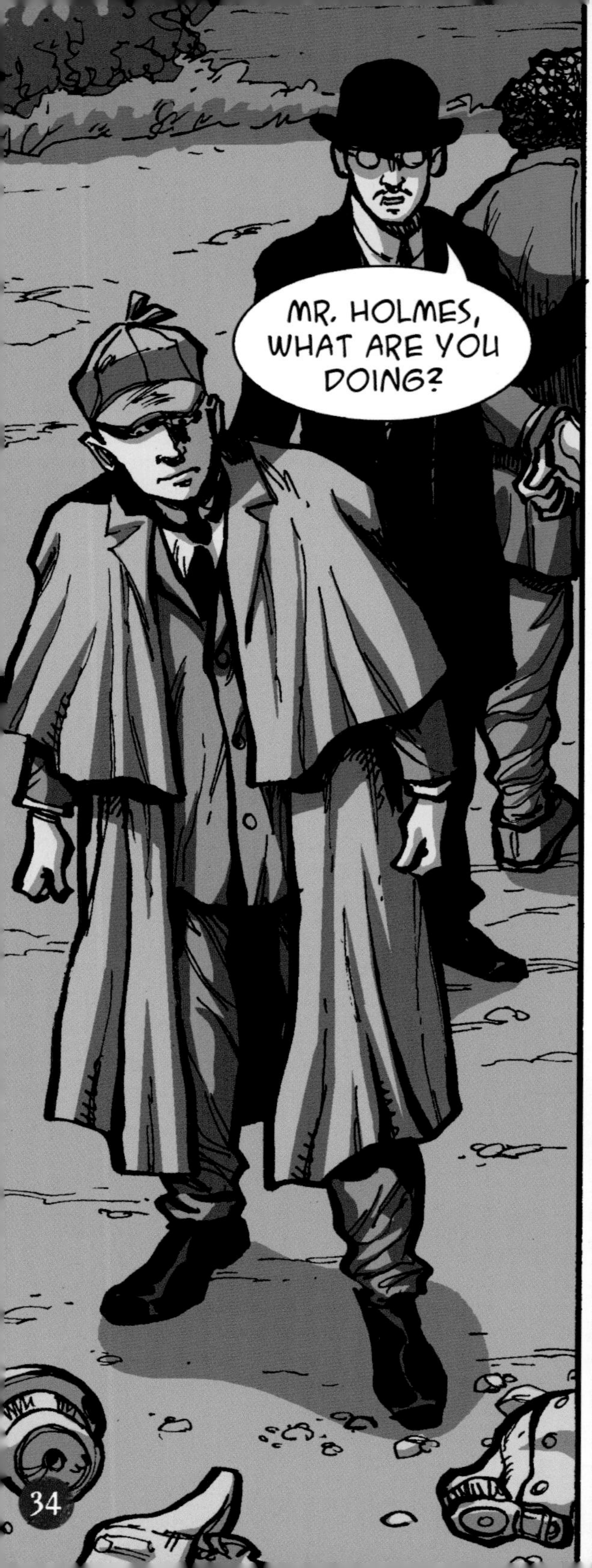
MR. HOLMES, WHAT ARE YOU DOING?

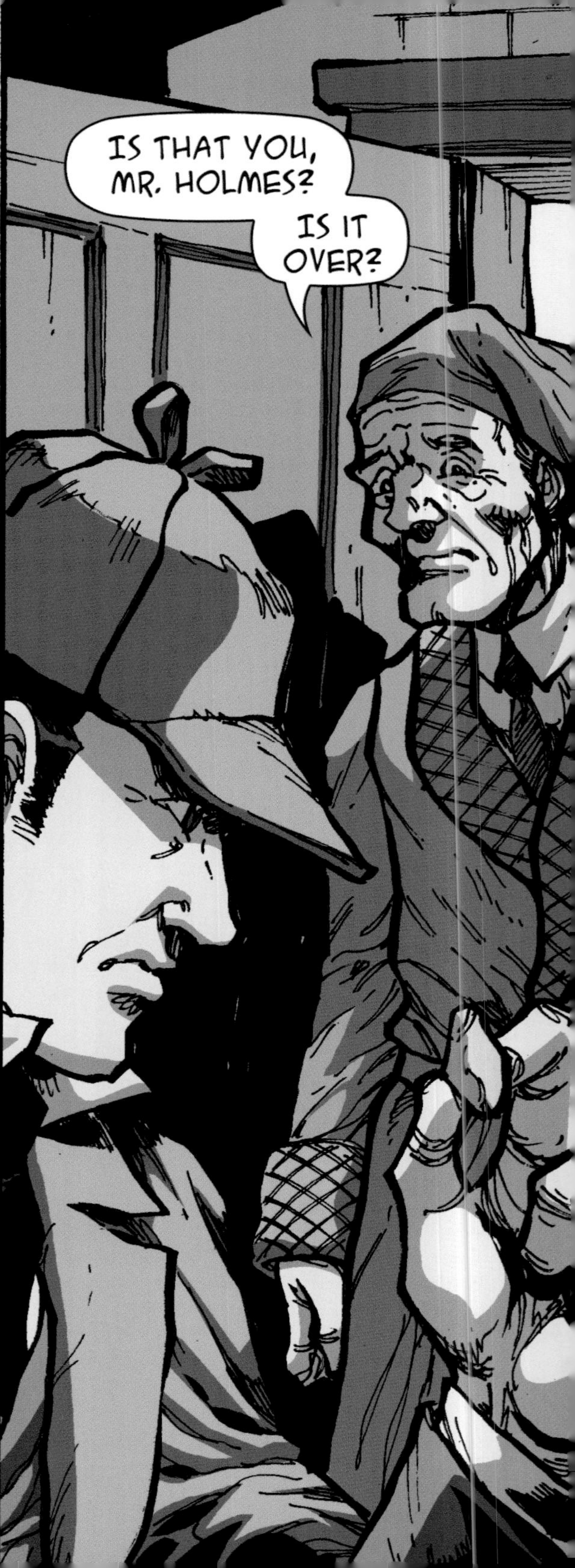
IS THAT YOU, MR. HOLMES?
IS IT OVER?

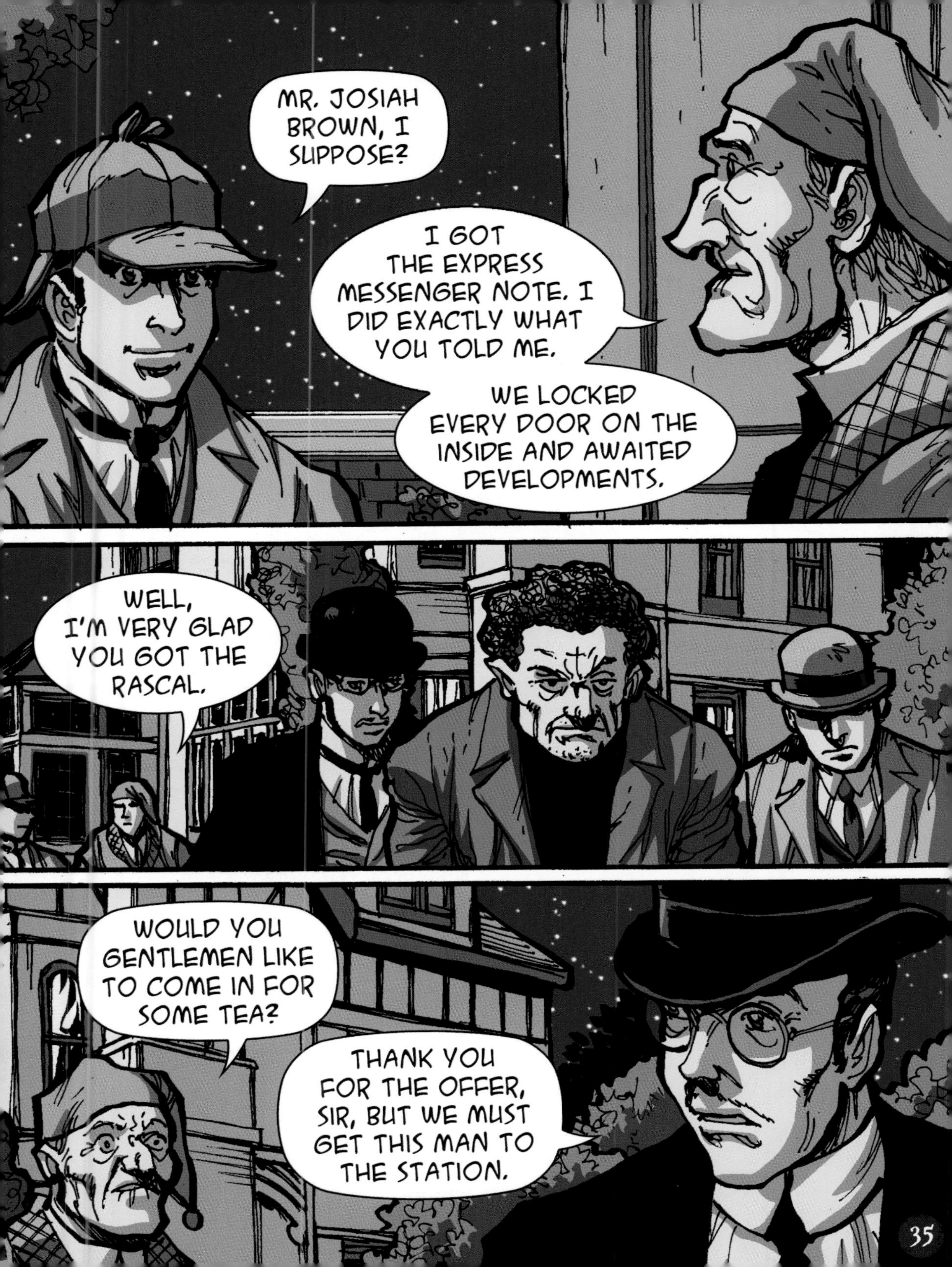
MR. JOSIAH BROWN, I SUPPOSE?
I GOT THE EXPRESS MESSENGER NOTE. I DID EXACTLY WHAT YOU TOLD ME.
WE LOCKED EVERY DOOR ON THE INSIDE AND AWAITED DEVELOPMENTS.
WELL, I'M VERY GLAD YOU GOT THE RASCAL.
WOULD YOU GENTLEMEN LIKE TO COME IN FOR SOME TEA?
THANK YOU FOR THE OFFER, SIR, BUT WE MUST GET THIS MAN TO THE STATION.

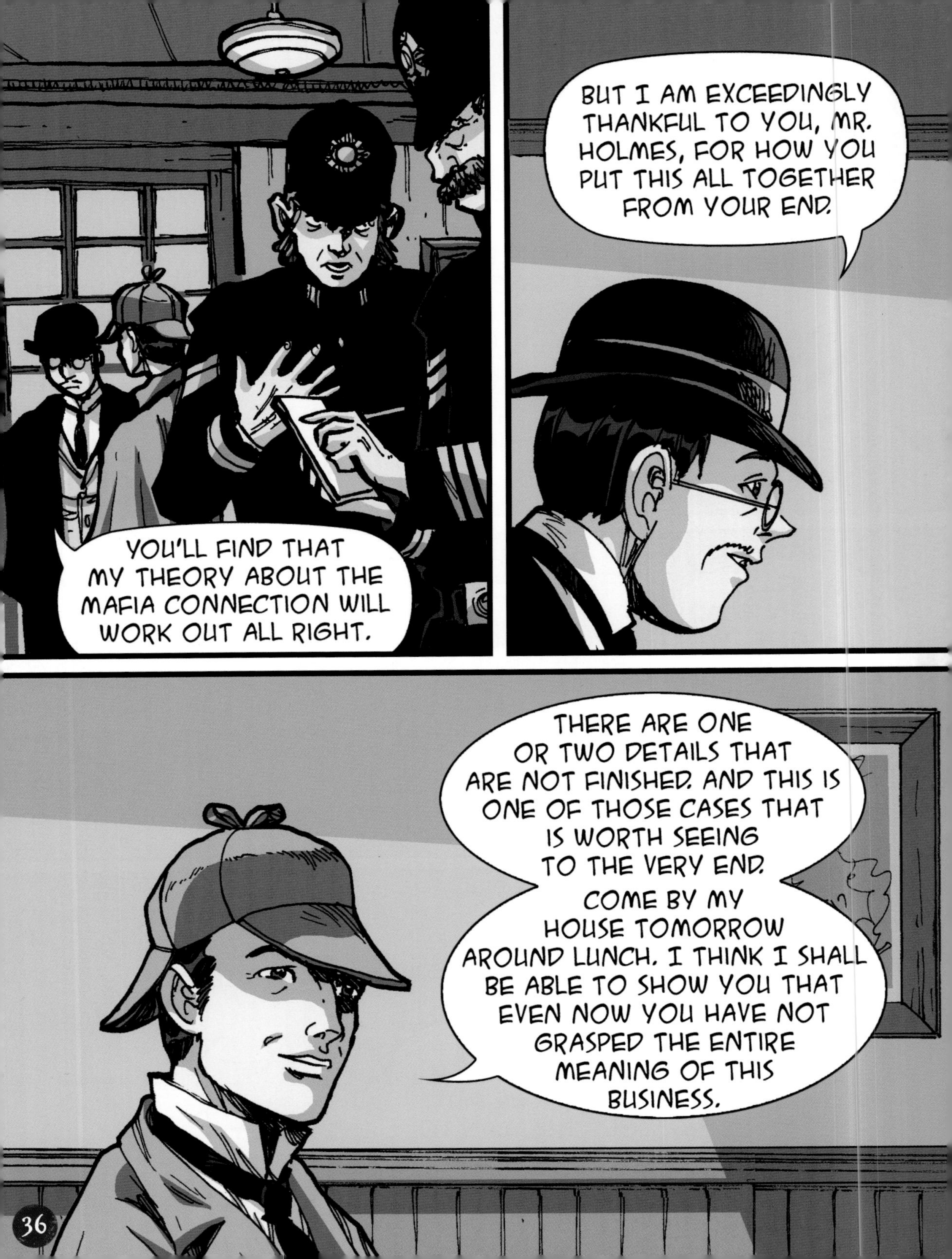
YOU'LL FIND THAT MY THEORY ABOUT THE MAFIA CONNECTION WILL WORK OUT ALL RIGHT.
BUT I AM EXCEEDINGLY THANKFUL TO YOU, MR. HOLMES, FOR HOW YOU PUT THIS ALL TOGETHER FROM YOUR END.
THERE ARE ONE OR TWO DETAILS THAT ARE NOT FINISHED. AND THIS IS ONE OF THOSE CASES THAT IS WORTH SEEING TO THE VERY END.
COME BY MY HOUSE TOMORROW AROUND LUNCH. I THINK I SHALL BE ABLE TO SHOW YOU THAT EVEN NOW YOU HAVE NOT GRASPED THE ENTIRE MEANING OF THIS BUSINESS.

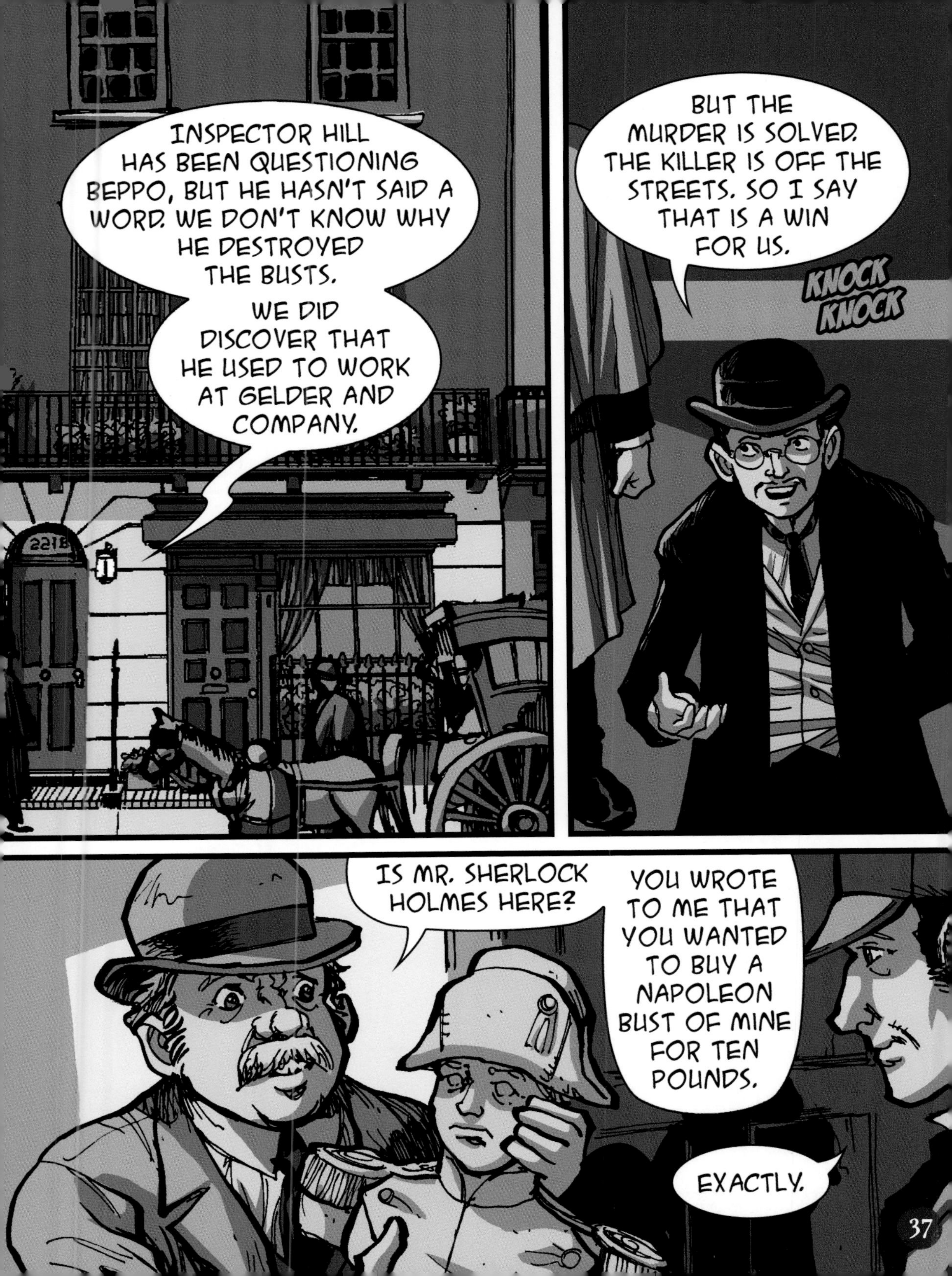
INSPECTOR HILL HAS BEEN QUESTIONING BEPPO, BUT HE HASN'T SAID A WORD. WE DON'T KNOW WHY HE DESTROYED THE BUSTS.
WE DID DISCOVER THAT HE USED TO WORK AT GELDER AND COMPANY.
221B
BUT THE MURDER IS SOLVED. THE KILLER IS OFF THE STREETS. SO I SAY THAT IS A WIN FOR US.
KNOCK KNOCK
IS MR. SHERLOCK HOLMES HERE?
YOU WROTE TO ME THAT YOU WANTED TO BUY A NAPOLEON BUST OF MINE FOR TEN POUNDS.
EXACTLY.

I WAS VERY MUCH SURPRISED AT YOUR LETTER. I COULD NOT IMAGINE HOW YOU KNEW THAT I OWNED SUCH A THING.
THE HARDING BROTHERS SAID THAT THEY HAD SOLD YOU THEIR LAST COPY. MR. HARDING GAVE ME YOUR ADDRESS.
I ONLY PAID 15 SHILLINGS FOR THE BUST. I THINK YOU OUGHT TO KNOW THAT BEFORE I TAKE TEN POUNDS FROM YOU.
I APPRECIATE YOUR HONESTY, MR. SANDEFORD. BUT I HAVE NAMED THAT PRICE, SO I INTEND TO STICK TO IT.
YOU WILL KINDLY SIGN THIS PAPER, MR. SANDEFORD, IN THE PRESENCE OF THESE WITNESSES.
IT IS SIMPLY TO SAY THAT YOU TRANSFER EVERY POSSIBLE RIGHT THAT YOU EVER HAD IN THE BUST TO ME.

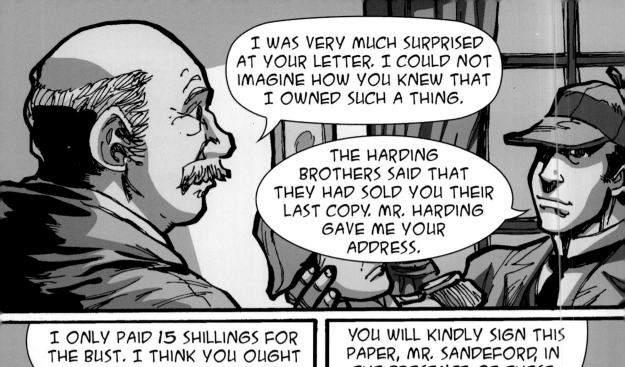

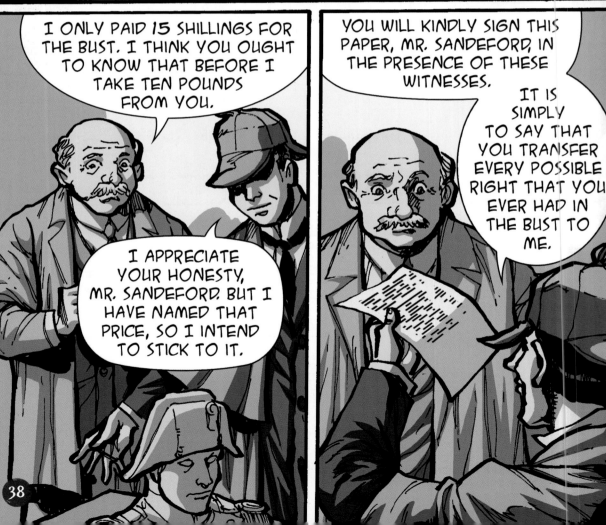

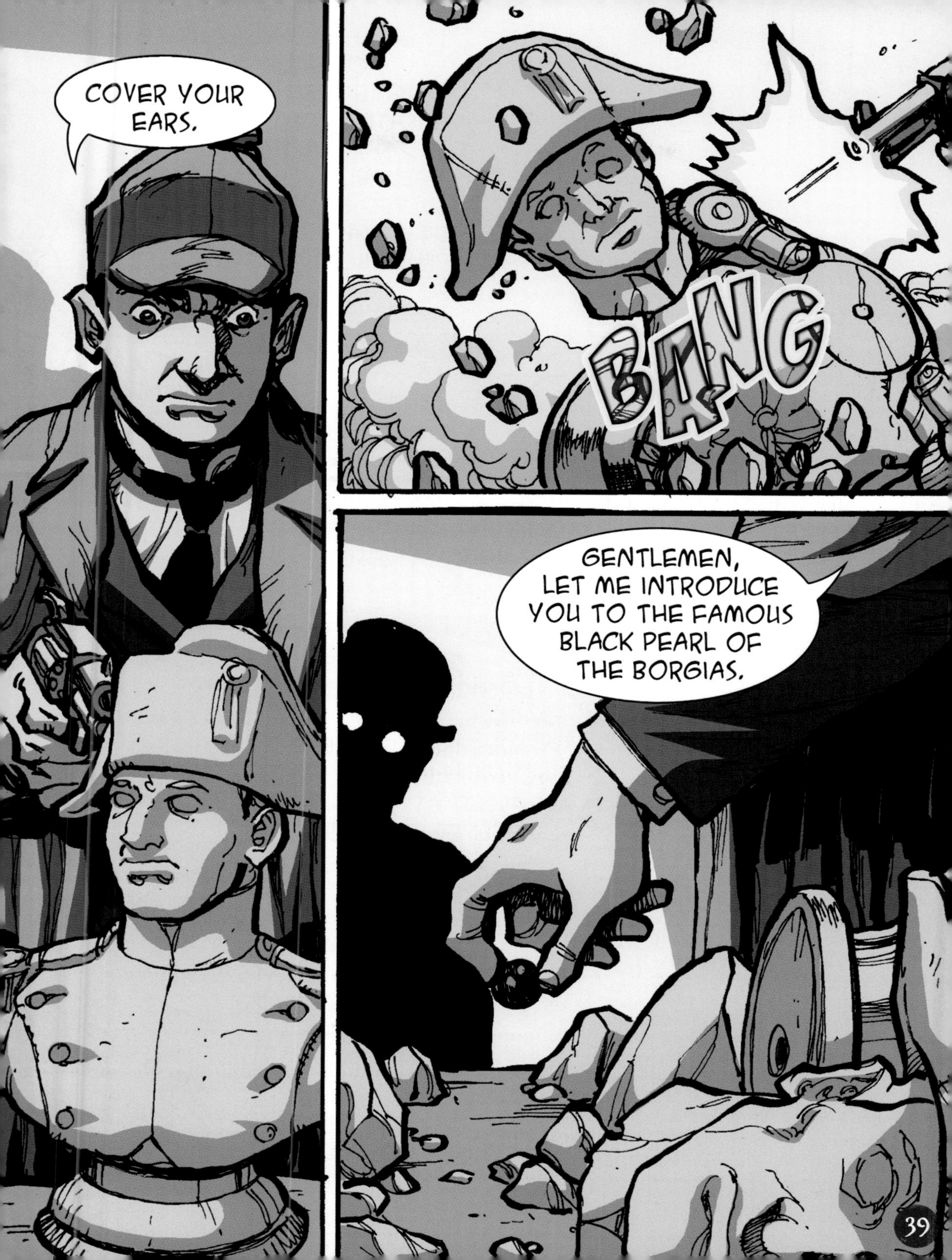
COVER YOUR EARS.
BANG
GENTLEMEN, LET ME INTRODUCE YOU TO THE FAMOUS BLACK PEARL OF THE BORGIAS.

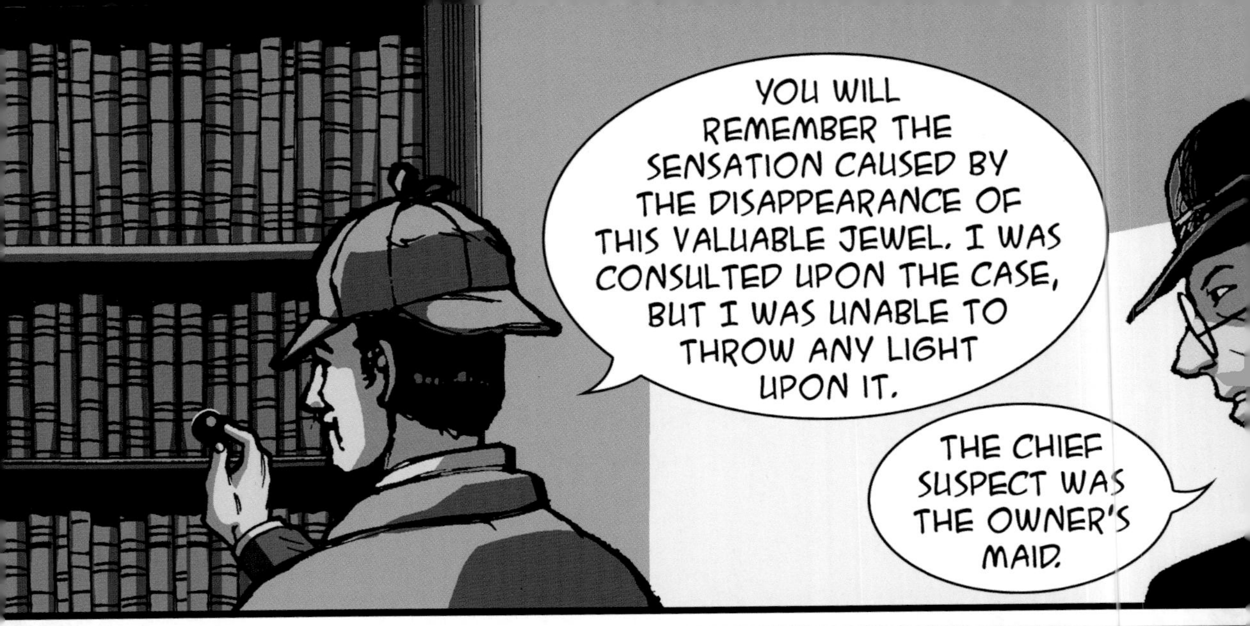
YOU WILL REMEMBER THE SENSATION CAUSED BY THE DISAPPEARANCE OF THIS VALUABLE JEWEL. I WAS CONSULTED UPON THE CASE, BUT I WAS UNABLE TO THROW ANY LIGHT UPON IT.
THE CHIEF SUSPECT WAS THE OWNER'S MAID.

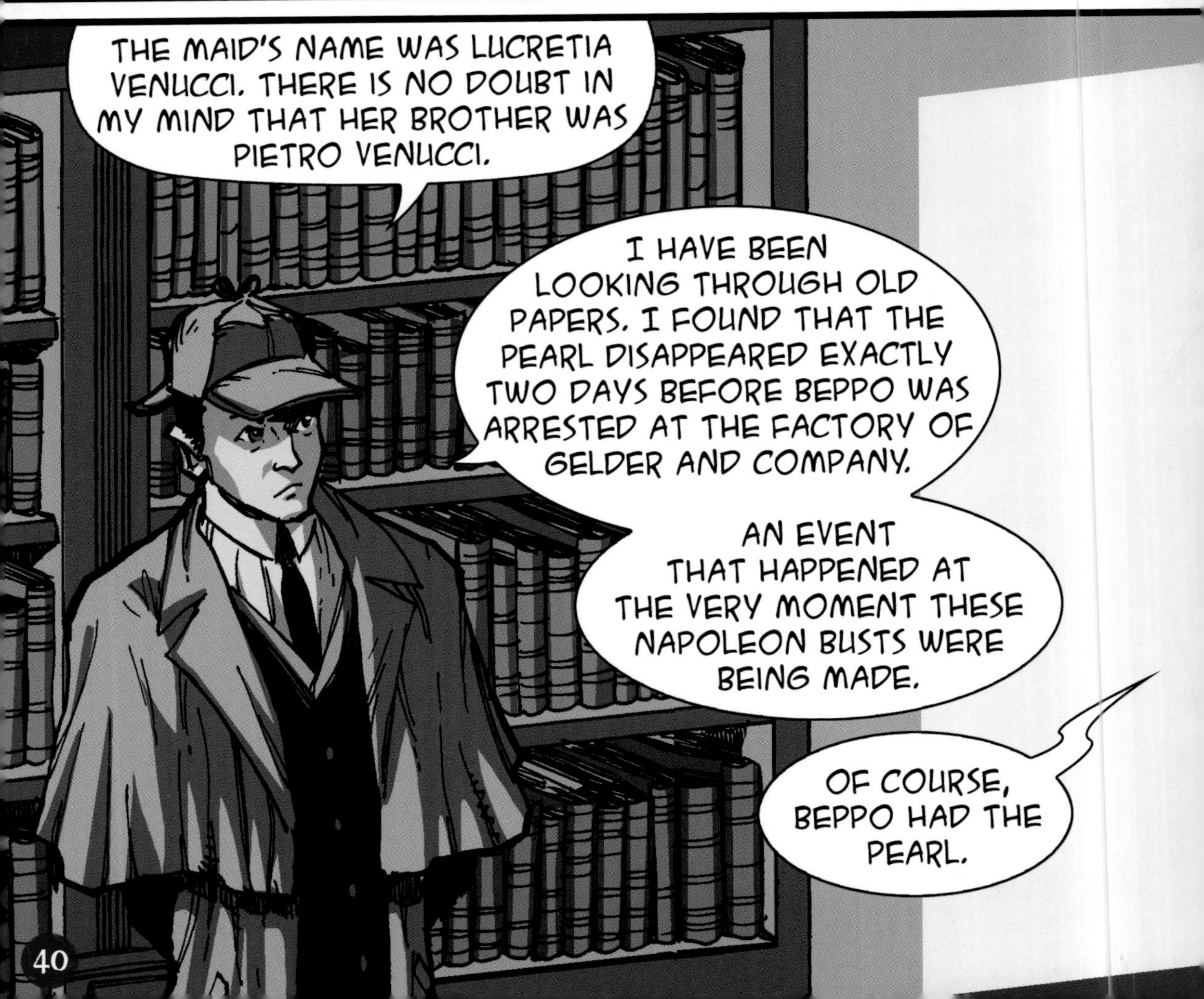
THE MAID'S NAME WAS LUCRETIA VENUCCI. THERE IS NO DOUBT IN MY MIND THAT HER BROTHER WAS PIETRO VENUCCI.
I HAVE BEEN LOOKING THROUGH OLD PAPERS. I FOUND THAT THE PEARL DISAPPEARED EXACTLY TWO DAYS BEFORE BEPPO WAS ARRESTED AT THE FACTORY OF GELDER AND COMPANY.
AN EVENT THAT HAPPENED AT THE VERY MOMENT THESE NAPOLEON BUSTS WERE BEING MADE.
OF COURSE, BEPPO HAD THE PEARL.

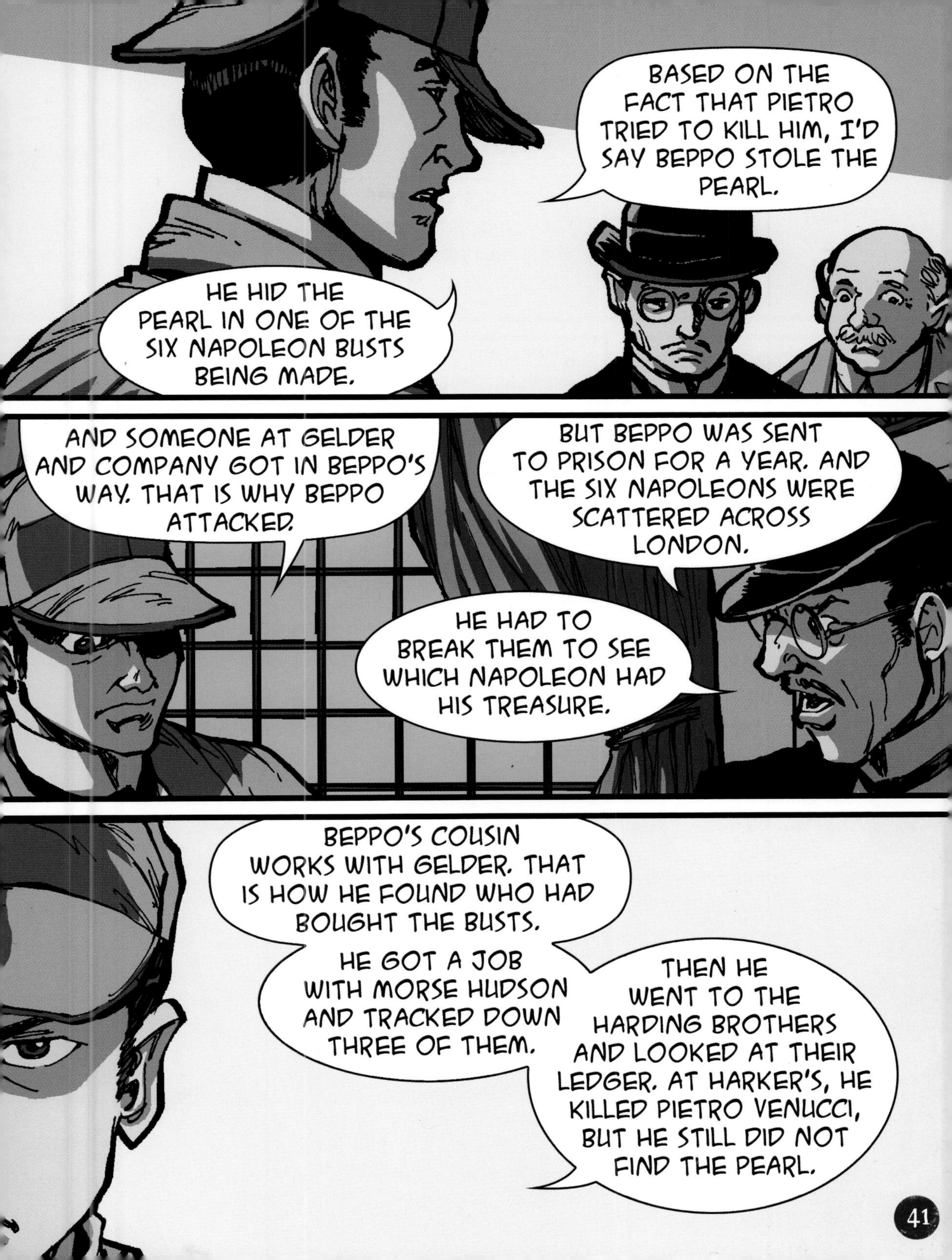
BASED ON THE FACT THAT PIETRO TRIED TO KILL HIM, I'D SAY BEPPO STOLE THE PEARL.
HE HID THE PEARL IN ONE OF THE SIX NAPOLEON BUSTS BEING MADE.
AND SOMEONE AT GELDER AND COMPANY GOT IN BEPPO'S WAY. THAT IS WHY BEPPO ATTACKED.
BUT BEPPO WAS SENT TO PRISON FOR A YEAR. AND THE SIX NAPOLEONS WERE SCATTERED ACROSS LONDON.
HE HAD TO BREAK THEM TO SEE WHICH NAPOLEON HAD HIS TREASURE.
BEPPO'S COUSIN WORKS WITH GELDER. THAT IS HOW HE FOUND WHO HAD BOUGHT THE BUSTS.
HE GOT A JOB WITH MORSE HUDSON AND TRACKED DOWN THREE OF THEM.
THEN HE WENT TO THE HARDING BROTHERS AND LOOKED AT THEIR LEDGER. AT HARKER'S, HE KILLED PIETRO VENUCCI, BUT HE STILL DID NOT FIND THE PEARL.

BUT IF VENUCCI KNEW BEPPO, WHY WAS HE CARRYING HIS PHOTOGRAPH?

SO HE COULD ASK STRANGERS, "HAVE YOU SEEN THIS MAN?"

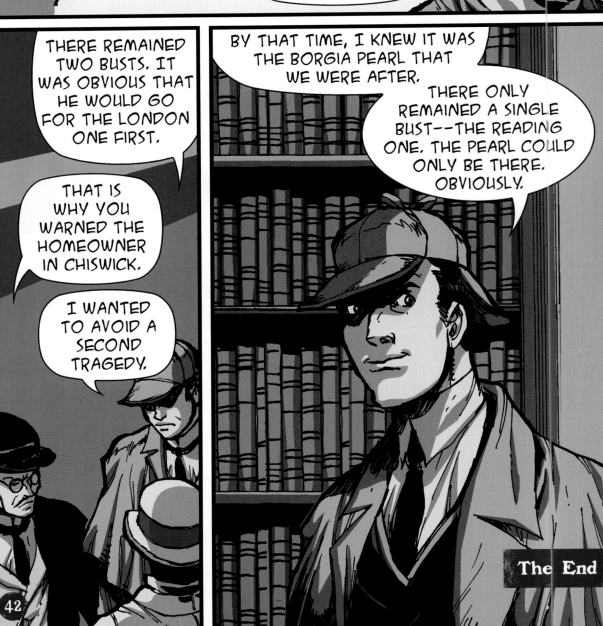

THERE REMAINED TWO BUSTS. IT WAS OBVIOUS THAT HE WOULD GO FOR THE LONDON ONE FIRST.

THAT IS WHY YOU WARNED THE HOMEOWNER IN CHISWICK.

I WANTED TO AVOID A SECOND TRAGEDY.

BY THAT TIME, I KNEW IT WAS THE BORGIA PEARL THAT WE WERE AFTER.

THERE ONLY REMAINED A SINGLE BUST--THE READING ONE. THE PEARL COULD ONLY BE THERE. OBVIOUSLY.

The End

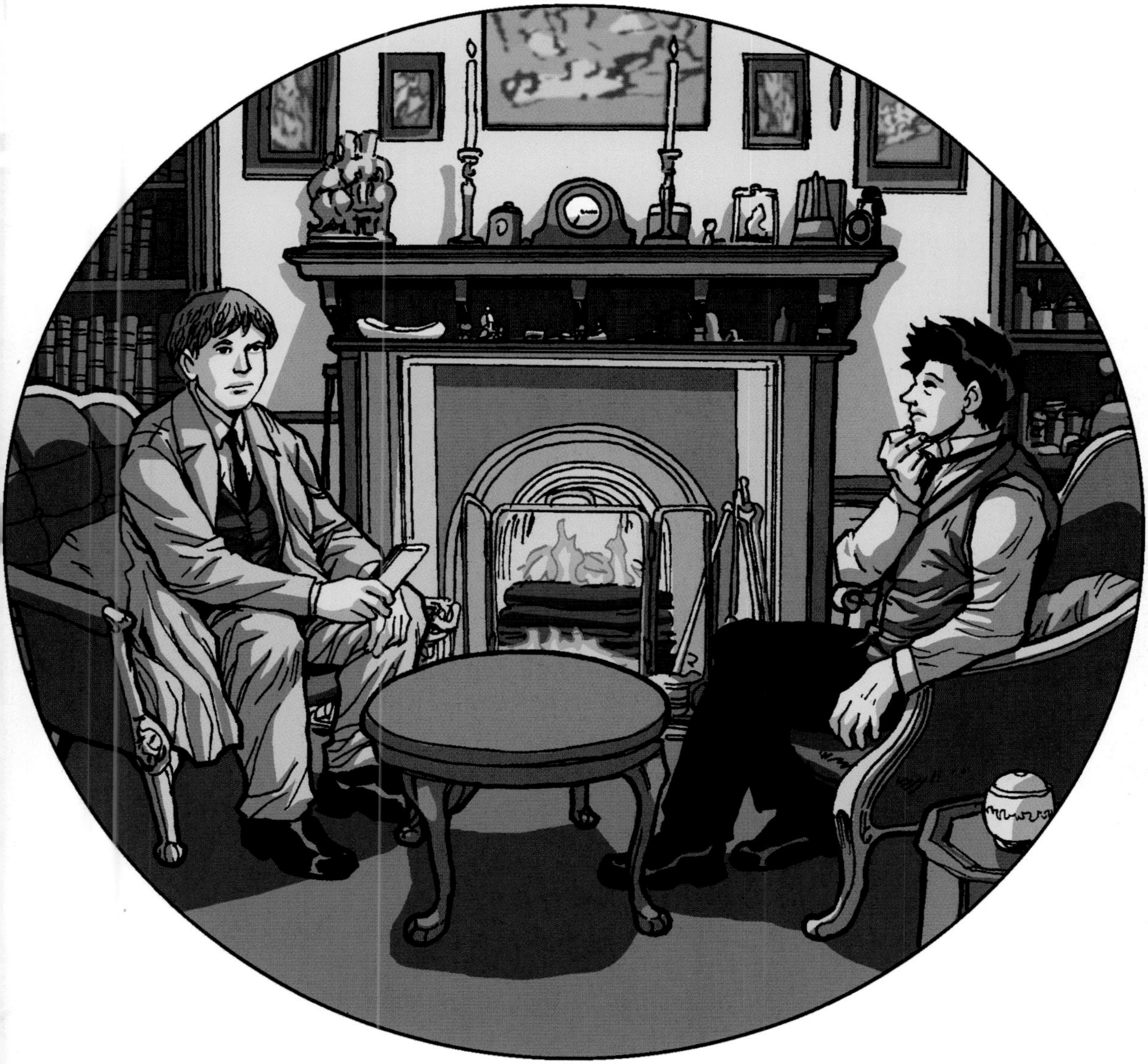

How to Draw
Dr. John Watson
by Ben Dunn

Step 1: Use a pencil to draw a simple framework. You can start with a stick figure! Then add circles, ovals, and cylinders to get the basic form. Getting the simple shapes in place is the beginning to solving any great case.

Step 2: Time to add to Watson's look. Use the shapes you started with to fill in his clothes. Use guidelines to add circles for the eyes. And don't forget to make sure the hat covers the head, not floats on top of it.

Step 3: Now you can go in with a pen and start inking Watson. Fill in all the details and fix any mistakes. Let the ink dry to avoid smudges, then erase any pencil marks. Watson is ready for some color, so grab your markers and get started!

Glossary

bust - a statue of a person's head and shoulders.
compromise - to reveal information to an enemy.
cutthroat - a killer.
identify - to recognize and name.
intrigue - to cause interest in.
lunatic - someone who is insane or mad.
Mafia - a secret criminal society of Italy.
motive - a reason that causes someone to act.
pound - the basic unit of money in the United Kingdom.
practical - being most useful or the best course of action.
propose - to offer for consideration or acceptance.
shilling - a former British coin.
theory - an explanation of how or why something happens.
victim - someone who is hurt in an accident.

Web Sites

To learn more about Sir Arthur Conan Doyle, visit ABDO Group online at **www.abdopublishing.com**. Web sites about Doyle are featured on our Book Links page. These links are routinely monitored and updated to provide the most current information available.

About the Author

Arthur Conan Doyle was born on May 22, 1859, in Edinburgh, Scotland. He was the second of Charles Altamont and Mary Foley Doyle's ten children. In 1868, Doyle began his schooling in England. Eight years later, he returned to Scotland.

Upon his return, Doyle entered the University of Edinburgh's medical school, where he became a doctor in 1885. That year, he married Louisa Hawkins. Together they had two children.

While a medical student, Doyle was impressed when his professor observed the tiniest details of a patient's condition. Doyle later wrote stories where his most famous character, Sherlock Holmes, used this same technique to solve mysteries. Holmes first appeared in A Study in Scarlet in 1887 and was immediately popular.

Between 1887 and 1927, Doyle wrote 66 stories and 3 novels about Holmes. He also wrote other fiction and nonfiction novels throughout his life. In 1902, Doyle was knighted for his work in a field hospital in the South African War. Four years later, Louisa died. Doyle married Jean Leckie in 1907, and they had three children together.

Sir Arthur Conan Doyle died on July 7, 1930, in Sussex, England. Today, Doyle's famous character, Sherlock Holmes, is honored with societies around the world that pay tribute to the detective.

Additional Works

A Study in Scarlet (1887)

The Mystery of Cloomber (1889)

The Firm of Girdlestone (1890)

The White Company (1891)

The Adventures of Sherlock Holmes (1891-92)

The Memoirs of Sherlock Holmes (1892-93)

Round the Red Lamp (1894)

The Stark Munro Letters (1895)

The Great Boer War (1900)

The Hound of the Baskervilles (1901-02)

The Return of Sherlock Holmes (1903-04)

Through the Magic Door (1907)

The Crime of the Congo (1909)

The Coming of the Fairies (1922)

Memories and Adventures (1924)

The Case-Book of Sherlock Holmes (1921-1927)

About the Adapters

Author

Vincent Goodwin earned his BA in Drama and Communications from Trinity University in San Antonio. He is the writer of three plays as well as the cowriter of the comic book *Pirates vs. Ninjas II.* Goodwin is also an accomplished journalist, having won several awards for his work as a columnist and reporter.

Illustrator

Ben Dunn founded Antarctic Press, one of the largest comic companies in the United States. His works appear in Marvel and Image comics. He is best known for his series *Ninja High School* and *Warrior Nun Areala.*